No
Pretty Picture

No
Pretty Picture

Maud Hawk
Wright
and
Villa's Raid
on Columbus

A Novel
Based on
Historical Facts

Michael Archie Hays

Sunstone
Press

Santa Fe

Sunstone books may be purchased for educational, business, or sales promotional use.
For information please write: Special Markets Department, Sunstone Press,
P.O. Box 2321, Santa Fe, New Mexico 87504-2321.

Book and cover design › Vicki Ahl
Body typeface › Garamond Pro
Printed on acid-free paper
eBook 978-1-61139-463-4

Library of Congress Cataloging-in-Publication Data

Names: Hays, Michael Archie, 1951- author.
Title: No pretty picture : Maud Hawk Wright and Villa's Raid on Columbus; a novel based on
historical facts / by Michael Archie Hays.
Description: Sante Fe : Sunstone Press, 2016.
Identifiers: LCCN 2016017534 (print) | LCCN 2016021284 (ebook) | ISBN
    9781632931023 (softcover : alk. paper) | ISBN 9781611394634
Subjects: LCSH: Villa, Pancho, 1878-1923--Fiction. | Medders, Maud,
    1889-1980--Fiction. | Revolutionaries--Mexico--Fiction. | Women--Fiction.
    | Kidnapping--Fiction. | Mexico--History--Revolution, 1910-1920--Fiction.
    | GSAFD: Historical fiction.
Classification: LCC PS3608.A9854 N6 2016 (print) | LCC PS3608.A9854 (ebook) |
    DDC 813/.6--dc23
LC record available at https://lccn.loc.gov/2016017534

SUNSTONE PRESS IS COMMITTED TO MINIMIZING OUR ENVIRONMENTAL IMPACT ON THE PLANET.
THE PAPER USED IN THIS BOOK IS FROM RESPONSIBLY MANAGED FORESTS. OUR PRINTER HAS RECEIVED CHAIN OF CUSTODY
(COC) CERTIFICATION FROM: THE FOREST STEWARDSHIP COUNCIL™ (FSC®), PROGRAMME FOR THE ENDORSEMENT OF FOREST
CERTIFICATION™ (PEFC™), AND THE SUSTAINABLE FORESTRY INITIATIVE® (SFI®).
THE FSC® COUNCIL IS A NON-PROFIT ORGANIZATION, PROMOTING THE ENVIRONMENTALLY APPROPRIATE, SOCIALLY BENEFICIAL
AND ECONOMICALLY VIABLE MANAGEMENT OF THE WORLD'S FORESTS. FSC® CERTIFICATION IS RECOGNIZED INTERNATIONALLY
AS A RIGOROUS ENVIRONMENTAL AND SOCIAL STANDARD FOR RESPONSIBLE FOREST MANAGEMENT.

WWW.SUNSTONEPRESS.COM
SUNSTONE PRESS / POST OFFICE BOX 2321 / SANTA FE, NM 87504-2321 /USA
(505) 988-4418 / ORDERS ONLY (800) 243-5644 / FAX (505) 988-1025

For my wife, Tamra
And the people of Mountainair, New Mexico

The author thanks Marla Lovato, Don Harvey, Biddie McMath, Oscar Medders and the librarians of the public library of Columbus, NM, for their help with research, and Maggie Hays and Claudio Dimas for their help with Spanish.

PREFACE

When my wife and I first moved to Mountainair, New Mexico, living there during the summer while we taught abroad, she came across an entry in a small book about the town, a collection of oral history. She said, "Get a load of this," and read a few paragraphs about a local woman, who, when young, was kidnapped by Pancho Villa's army and witnessed Villa's ill-fated raid on a New Mexican border town, Columbus. I was astonished. I told her that it struck me as a perfect story to develop into a novel. "Well, then, here's the kicker," she said. The last line of the story stated that the woman, Maud Medders, was survived by a number of people, one of whom was our next-door neighbor. "Time to get to work," I said. My poor neighbor. My wife and I were sitting on our front patio having drinks when she pulled up into her driveway, returning from a long camping trip. She had hardly closed her car door when I started bombarding her with questions. "All right," she said. "Let me at least get cleaned up first."

People in town were generally helpful, mainly describing Maud as a friendly elderly lady who had died decades ago. But older folks remembered her as a remarkably tough and skillful horsewoman who herded cattle, roped calves, and would ride the trails of the Manzano Mountains into her late years. In one case, she was remembered as a little tricky. Her great-grandson described how she would make a batch of cookies, the odor of which would draw him into the kitchen. By the time he had earned access to the cookies, he had stacked wood and drawn water for her.

But of her adventure with Pancho Villa, most knew little, only that it was hard going. Not much of a talker to begin with, Maud hadn't said much about it.

Others sources helped, especially articles from the 1916 New York Times, provided by the kind staff of the Columbus, NM public library. The best source of information, provided by our neighbor, was Maud's description of the ordeal as recounted and typed up by some of her friends. Everything she described and everything she said to her captors found a place in the following novel.

JANUARY 11, 1916

The train howled to a stop before it reached the derailed car on the tracks. Rebels stood quietly above the train on an incline beside the tracks. After a few minutes, three Americans left the back door of their car to see what had stopped the train. The rebels shot at them, killing two as they stepped off the platform. The third American fell and rolled away, hiding behind some mesquite.

A few of the raiders were on horseback, drawing up alongside the locomotive, lifting their rifle barrels to the drivers. One rebel shouted an order, "Hernandez. *Encuéntralos*." Hernandez nodded, and with others galloped along the passenger cars, looking through the windows.

They rode the length of the train and returned to a car near the engine. Hernandez reared his horse and yelled, "*Coronel, aquí están,*" pointing at the car. Four of the rebels dismounted and entered the car at each end, front and rear, pulling their sombreros off their heads. They worked the levers of their Winchesters, and one of the rebels shot a hole through roof and shouted at the clamoring passengers to be silent.

The leader of the rebels followed his men into the car and passing them, moved down the aisle, perusing the passengers, nodding to women, murmuring formal greetings to the men. He saw Hernandez taking money off a Mexican passenger. "*No,* Hernandez, *sólo de los gringos.*" Hernandez lowered his sword and returned the cash. Then stopping at a group of fifteen men in woolen suits, he said, "You are the gringo engineers for the Cusihuiriachic mine." A young man seated with the group translated. The engineers nodded, glancing at one another.

"Get off the train." The young man translated for the engineers. One of the engineers lurched toward the lead rebel but was met with a saber point to his chest. He sat back slowly. Another leaned forward to rise, but another threw his arm across his chest to stop him. "Who are you? You can't order us around. We are here by invitation of President Carranza."

The translator started to explain, but the man snarled. "I know why they are here. Tell them I am Pablo López, colonel of the Army of Pancho Villa, and I order them to get off the train." Another rebel stepped into the car, drew one bullet after another from his bandolier draped over his shoulder, and slipped them into the magazine of his rifle. The engineers stood up confusedly, and Hernandez tapped them with his sword toward the rear door of the car. He motioned to the rebels at the door to pat their coats for weapons.

As the gringos stepped off the car, rebels pulled them together to form a line facing the train. Indignant, confused, the gringos yelled and cursed at their captors. López followed the last gringo off the car steps and pushed him toward the line. He shouted an order and the rebels lined up, backs to the train, and raised their rifles and aimed. Some of the men in line blustered, spat curses. Some, their arms raised, pleaded. One fell to his knees in prayer, "Lord! Lord!" López then shouted to the Americans, "Take off your clothes. Tell them, translator. Tell them to take off their clothing."

The translator, bewildered, passed the message to the engineers. They looked at one another and slowly began to disrobe, keeping an eye on the firing squad before them. Soon they were standing in their underwear. López told the translator to take the clothes away and pile them near the train.

On López's command, the rebels shot off a round each, and half of the men in line, their legs and shoulders suddenly slack, dropped in place. The kneeling man toppled sidelong, open-eyed, a red black hole in his forehead. The remainder gaped in a mute, bewildered horror, at the bodies beside them. Then, after the click of levers, another round of shots dropped more men, and another round finished them.

López mounted his horse and rode up to the locomotive. He shouted over the engine's blasts of steam. The drivers nodded, and the locomotive lurched, clanking and screaming, forward, workers levering the derailed car back onto the tracks. As the train rolled slowly away, the rebels could see the passengers gawking through the windows at them and their carnage. One of the rebels cried out, "*¡Viva Villa! Viva la revolución!*" and the men around him repeated the cry for their audience.

Rebels picked through the pile of clothing, testing their feet against the boots of the dead, slipping belts around their waists, holding pants up for inspection. Some tried on their new clothes, but most tossed them on the back of their mounts. Hernandez used the point of his saber to lift a hat from the pile. He tossed it in the air, caught it with his free hand, and crammed it on his head, crushing its crown. Clownlike, he pleaded for mercy with high-pitched affectation, raising his arms, turning to each rebel. Laughing, the men returned to their scavenging, while Hernandez dropped the hat on the impassive face of its owner and pinned it with his sword. The bodies, denuded or reduced to their bloodied woolens, lay in grotesque shapes, their arms and legs sprawled.

The rebels lashed their new clothes to their saddles or stuffed them into sacks, and mounted their horses. After a few words between López and Hernandez, the raiders rode away together down the hillside away from the train.

The survivor of the raid, Thomas B. Holmes, had made his way back to El Paso and reported the slaughter. His report reached President Wilson, who promptly put the border on alert, giving authority to General John J. Pershing, headquartered at Fort Bliss, to place El Paso under martial law, both to prevent more of the increasing number of bandit raids on Americans and to prevent retaliatory attacks on Mexicans. Staffed by the three hundred and fifty soldiers of the army's 13th Calvary, Camp Furlong in Columbus, New Mexico, was an outpost in that militarization.

MARCH 1, 1916

When the gringa stepped out of her house with a baby on her hip, Cervantes asked his lieutenant, "*¿Es ella?*"

Hernandez nodded. "*Creo que sí.*"

"*Órale, pues.* We'll take her."

The day was ending, a few grey clouds drifted along the western horizon, and a chilling breeze rolled through the highland pines when Cervantes and his men neared the Wrights' ranch. A couple of days earlier, they had raided nearby Colonias Juarez, collecting about a hundred head of cattle and scaring off dozens of the remaining *norteamericanos*. They were heading back to Villa's mountain camp, where thousands of Villistas were holed up waiting for supplies. Locals had informed the raiders that the gringo family had returned with cattle to the logging ranch months earlier, so Cervantes figured it made sense to relieve them of their herd on the way back to camp. The woman, they said, was an excellent horse-woman. As they approached the ranch, he rode around the edge of his men, splitting them into three groups, a half dozen to manage the cattle, a dozen to scour the hills of the ranch and drive new cattle down to the others, and the remainder to clear the house of its supplies.

When they rode up to her house, eight of them, a young woman stepped out the door smiling, holding her baby, thinking her husband had returned. Her face dropped when she saw in the twilight a group of riders gathered in front of her house, rifles laid across their laps, bandoliers draped from their chests and sombreros slouching heavily over their eyes. She backed up against the adobe wall of her house. Cervantes reined his horse closer to her and spoke politely.

"*Buenas tardes, Señora. Tal vez tenga algo que pueda comprar, algunas sobras de comida.* We are famished."

She wore a plain cotton dress. She frowned and squinted her small, grey eyes. Cervantes watched her think.

"I have some dinner for my husband and his hand. They'll be here shortly. It's not enough for all of you." Her Spanish was fluent, slowed by a drawl.

"*Gracias, Señora.* Perhaps you have something in your storeroom."

"*Lo siento, pero tenemos muy poco.* My husband and his hand went to Pearson for supplies. Maybe they will sell you something. I expect they'll be here any time now. Who are you?"

"*Coronel Cervantes, Señora, a su servicio, y* éstos *son mis hombres, mis compañeros.*"

"Soldiers? Are you from the garrison? Don't they feed you there?"

"Not well, *Señora.* Not recently."

Cervantes swung off his horse and held a hand up to his men. Exhausted, mute, they slid off their mounts and looked at the woman and her baby. Cervantes nodded to one of them to join him. The woman was standing in front of her door. The baby whimpered, and she hiked him to her breast.

"And what do you call yourself?"

"Maud. Maud Hawk Wright. My husband is Ed Wright. Like I said, he'll be back here with his men any time now. I reckon it'd be more fitting for you all to wait outside until they arrive."

Cervantes looked at her flatly. "It would be more fitting for you to do as I tell you."

Maud narrowed her eyes at him. "You're Carranza's men. You don't need anything from me. You can reach the garrison by midnight."

Cervantes laughed. He had raided the Wrights' ranch because gringos owned it. He had done it before. He was in the squad that had cleared the Wrights out years ago, when he was raiding cattle for Carranza, when Carranza was a revolutionary. Now Carranza was president, but Cervantes was still a revolutionary, a colonel for Villa.

Why did these people return, the Wrights, he wondered. Why is it so hard to get *gringos* to leave Mexico alone? This new wave of attacks differed from previous raids because this surge, brutal and sudden, was led by Villa. Villa knew what worked: give the *norteamericanos* a clear picture of their future if they stayed in Mexico. Surely this young woman, her jaw now set against them, had heard about the new raids and executions.

"Perhaps we're not with the army. Now please step aside."

A woman in a peasant dress stepped out and joined Maud under the porch, standing next to her. *"¿Qué está pasando, Señora?"*

"Una incursión, Maria. Another bunch of criminals. Where is your Augustin?"

"Ay, no sé, Señora. I haven't seen him."

Cervantes gazed at her. He placed his hand gently against Maud's side and nudged her away from her door.

"Hernandez, *ven conmigo.* We'll see for ourselves." One of the riders, rat-faced and chinless, walked into the the kitchen behind him. The room smelled warm with cooking beans. A pot simmered on the wood stove, and tomatoes and onions, half chopped, lay beside a knife on a table. Maud entered the kitchen, the baby whimpering in her arms, and stood at the table. Maria followed her in. Hernandez scooped out a spoonful of beans and blew on them, leaning over the stove.

"Watch her." Cervantes searched shelves for supplies. Hernandez took a bowl from the counter, filled it with beans, and leaned against the counter, smiling at Maud. *"Que bueno."*

Cervantes left the room to search the house. "Where's your store?" he shouted into the kitchen.

"Here, here in the kitchen. It's all we have." She pointed to a curtained cabinet under a pan of water. Cervantes strode across the room, and lifted the curtain with his saber. There were a few bags, some oats and some corn meal. He pulled them out into the kitchen floor. Maud reached toward the knife on the table. Hernandez lurched toward her, throwing the bowl aside, and slammed his hand on her wrist against the table top. He drew his body close and exhaled on her neck until she released the knife. She twisted away from him and held the baby with both arms.

Maria cried, "Please, *Señora*. They will kill you."

Cervantes laughed. "*Cálmese, Señora* Maud. Calm yourself. Your man, you say he'll be here soon with more?"

When Ed and Frank rode up to the gate of the ranch, they could see the traffic of the riders. They had already passed a gang they did not know tending to some cattle down the road, and on the hillside, they could see in the grey of twilight more riders herding Wright cattle down to the road. Without a word, Ed spurred his horse toward the house, while Frank urged speed from the mules, loaded with sacks of grain and meal. Around the porch of the house, Ed could see men, bandoliers across their chests, sombreros slung against their backs, milling around their horses. Some had already drawn on him by the time he reached the adobe.

Ed lifted his palms to them, grabbed his saddle horn, and threw his leg around the horse to dismount so quickly that the raiders clicked their rifle hammers and raised their aim. Several turned their aim to Frank as he rode up, tugging at reins of the lumbering animals behind him. He raised his hands, stood in his stirrups and slowly turned and lowered himself off his horse.

Ed nodded to the gunmen, and keeping his hands up and away from his body, shouted out, "Where's my wife? Maud, Maud, where are you?"

One of the gunmen drew closer to Ed and shouted a warning to Cervantes. Cervantes looked out the door. "Let him in. Leave the other outside and watch him. Search their horses for rifles."

Some of the men were already pulling bags off the animals. "Leave them. We'll keep the mules. *Señor* Ed? Enter please."

Ed rushed into the kitchen followed by a gunman, now pointing a pistol to Ed's back. Maud was at the table, clutching the baby on her lap, sitting with Maria. Hernandez looked at him over a spoonful of beans from the pot, and Cervantes motioned to a chair at the table. "I am Colonel Cervantes. We have been waiting for you, *Señor* Ed."

Ed pulled a chair up to the table across from Maud. "This looks bad."

"We'll be all right, Ed."

"No, this is bad, Maud. This is worse than the last time." He reached over and patted the baby on the head. "Johnnie all right?"

"Jittery, just like me, but he ain't crying."

Frank stumbled into the room, pushed from behind by a raider. "Goddamn it. I hate these sons of bitches," he muttered as sat himself down at the table.

Maud passed Johnnie to Maria and spoke to them quietly, hardly moving her lips. She pointed with her chin to their rifle, leaning against the corner.

"Is there something we can do?"

"No, Maud. No. There's a whole band of them out there.

Frank agreed. "They got the cattle, maybe all of it."

"I don't think I can sit here and let this happen again."

"Jesus, Maud. This is bad enough. Let's not get ourselves killed."

"It's true, Maud." Frank said. "They're all over the place."

Cervantes pushed a clay pot off a shelf, and it smashed on the floor, spilling corn meal on the floor. "Put your hands on the table. You, Ed. And you, the boy. Hands on the table."

"What did he say?"

"He wants to see your hands."

Maria took a jagged breath and squeezed Johnnie. Maud saw that her cheeks were wet with crying. "Everything will be all right, Maria. Augustin will be fine. We've gone through this before, remember?"

Cervantes smashed another bowl. He talked to Hernandez a moment then came to the table. "Ed, come with me. Boy, you stay here with the women."

Ed stood. "I'll be right back, Maud." He watched Cervantes leave the house. Cervantes turned at the door. "I said, come." He smiled and motioned out the door with his head. Ed followed him outside.

"Show me where to feed my horse." Cervantes mounted his horse. Ed stood still.

Ed was slow to move, so Cervantes pulled a rifle from his saddle holster. He aimed it at Ed's chest. Ed pulled himself on to his horse.

"Cut some rope. Tie him up." A raider jerked Ed's arms behind him and lashed his wrists together.

"Now call your boy."

"The baby?"

"Not the baby, fool. Your worker."

"There's no need. You have the food. You have the stock. What else is there?"

"Call him."

Ed breathed. "Frank."

"Loud."

"Frank, come on out here, will you."

Frank stepped out of the house, "Yeah?" He backed against the wall when he saw Ed, mounted, his arms hidden behind him. "Hey, hey," he shouted in confusion, while some raiders shoved him toward Cervantes.

"Get on the horse, Frank," Cervantes shouted.

"I'm sorry, Frankie. I'm sorry."

"Get on the horse with Ed."

"I'm sorry, Frank."

"No problem, Ed. Goddam, I hate these bastards." Ed pulled his boot out of his stirrup. Frank stepped into the stirrup and mounted the horse behind Ed.

"Tie him up." The raider roped Frank's hands. Cervantes turned his horse toward Ed's, grabbed his reins, and led them away from the house. He took them as far as the gate and turned the reins over to another raider. In the gathering darkness, Augustin was sitting by a post, his head on his knees, his hands tied behind him. On the other side of the gate, a few raiders herded the last of the Wrights' cattle down the road. Cervantes joined them.

A streak of pink and orange clouds lay across the western hills, and a cold breeze blew from the east. Ed turned in his saddle and saw Maud holding Johnnie, standing outside the house, lit from the lamps within. Maria joined her. Maud looked for them and saw them by the gate, bound. She gathered her dress up with her free hand and ran to them. Johnnie was crying over her shoulder.

"What are they doing? You're a prisoner?" She was out of breath.

"There's Augustin, tell Maria he's safe."

"They're going to kill you, Ed. They're going to kill you both." Her eyes were wild.

"I reckon she's right, Ed. I don't think we're long," Frank muttered.

Cervantes walked to them and took Maud by the arm. "*Cállese, Señora*. Go back to the house." He pulled his saber to guide her.

"Go on inside now, Maud. It's too cold for the baby out here. I reckon everything will be all right if we just play along."

Cervantes yanked on her arm, but Maud stood planted, twisting around to Ed.

"Go now, Maud."

Stumbling behind Cervantes, Maud choked, calling her husband's name and crying. "Let go of me. Don't touch me!"

She jerked her arm free from Cervantes and screamed. "You've got everything. What more do you want? Let me alone. Let my husband go." Cervantes grabbed for her arm, and she swung it away from him. "Don't touch me." She shouted in English, "This ain't just. This ain't just. Leave us alone." She began to sob and fell to her knees, clutching the wailing baby to her chest. Cervantes watched her for a minute, and then pulled her up from under her arms. "Go inside."

In the kitchen, Cervantes pushed her on to a chair at the table with Maria. He walked outside. Maud's eyes were red. Maria crossed herself. "I don't know what they're going to do with the men. They got Augustin out there on the ground." They fell silent, and Maud patted and rubbed Johnnie's back, slightly rocking. "That's all right. That's all right, little mister." She closed her eyes and waited. Maria cried quietly.

In a while, Hernandez entered. Maud and Maria looked up at him. "*Señora*, your husband wants to see you. The Colonel says it is all right for you to see him now." Maud stood, holding Johnnie, and walked to the door. "Leave the baby, *Señora*. We will be back shortly." Maud put Johnnie in Maria's arms and walked out the door.

Hernandez lifted his foot into his stirrup, "Get on behind me."

"Where is he? Where's my husband?"

"*Allá*, behind that hill." He pointed with his chin. "Get up." He waved his hand behind him.

"You are out of your frail mind. I'm not getting on a horse with you."

"Good. Take that horse. I don't care. You're wasting time. Your husband needs to see you." He drew his sword from its scabbard.

"I don't trust this." She unlashed the reins of Frank's horse and mounted it.

"*No importa*. Come, let's go." He motioned with his sword.

They rode together a stretch up to a rise outside the gate. "I don't trust this. Where is he?"

"Right over there."

"Ed? Ed?"

There was no answer. "You're a filthy liar." She panicked and reined her horse around toward the house, but Hernandez pulled in front of her. "Get out of my way. I want my baby."

"You are coming with us."

"No, I'm not. I am going to my baby."

"*El Coronel* has given your child to the other woman."

Maud heaved for breath and slid off her horse. She dashed for the house, screaming, "No. No." Hernandez galloped in front of her. Maud ran into the flank of his horse and stumbled backward.

"Get back on your horse. We're leaving." Hernandez motioned an assurance into the dark toward Cervantes who was trotting toward them.

"*Señora*," Hernandez spoke kindly toward her. "Do what we say. Cervantes doesn't care who he kills. He will kill you soon, I think. Maybe I will kill you. Tomorrow in the morning, I think. We'll see what the *Generalisimo* wants."

Maud put her hands to her face, her shoulders heaving. Hernandez galloped his horse over to her, picked up its reins and led it to her. "Get on it." Maud complied. Hernandez kept the reins and led Maud back to house. Maria and Johnnie were gone. It was night, and the only light came from the lanterns inside. On horseback, Cervantes shouted orders, waving his saber. Raiders were swarming through the house, stripping it of goods. When their horses were loaded, a raider returned to the kitchen and knocked over a lantern, left the house and mounted his horse. Cervantes directed Maud to the front of the raiders. With his signal, they rode into the night, flames rising behind them.

MARCH 2

They rode the whole nearly moonless night, single file, through the low mountains of Chihuahua. Behind the raiders the cattle lumbered noisily, tailed by a few riders guarding Ed and Frank. In front of the train, Maud rode, slumped in her saddle, attended by an old man, a grey beard under a broad brim. Maud's middle was cramped from crying, and she held her shoulders against the cold. As the night drew toward dawn, she began to drift to sleep. Her head dropped forward, waking her, and waking, she felt such a wave of grief that she closed her eyes again for relief. The old man tugged his horse to hers and passed Maud a canteen.

"No." Maud turned away from him.

"*Por favor, Señora.*" He pushed it toward her again. She took it and sipped from it. She passed it back to him, but he put his hand up. "For you, *Señora.*" She found its strap and pulled it over her shoulder and let the canteen hang.

"You are cold?"

Maud didn't look up.

"Are you cold? Look, on your saddle, there is a *serape. Por favor, Señora*, put it on. You will feel better."

She looked behind her, found the pancho, pulled the leather ties loose and drew the thin wool over her head. It smelled thick of horse. She glanced at the old man.

"*¿Dónde está mi marido?*"

"I don't know, *Señora*. I am not the boss."

"Ed! Ed!" She shouted into the air. The old man put his hands up in horror. "Shh. *Por favor, cállase.*"

Hernandez rushed up from behind.

"Keep her quiet, Palo. If she screams, kill her. If you don't, I will kill you both."

"Where is my husband? I said, where is my husband?"

"Do you want to live? Shut up, woman." He wheeled his horse around. "Go, Palo. Keep her moving." Palo lifted his reins and gave Maud's horse a swat on its hindquarter. Her horse sauntered to its right and then returned to its slow pace.

Maud woke to a change in her horse's step. A cold breeze drifted from the east where light was crowning the mountains. Below them lay a wide drain, a canyon whose upper western edges were gilt with the dawn's light. Throughout the canyon along its thin stream, a few families camped, their shelters blankets and *serapes* pulled over low pines and poles. A few horses, tied to shrubs, tugged at clumps of grass. The old man motioned Maud to follow him down into the canyon, followed by Cervantes and the other raiders. The cattle bunched together noisily as they entered the *arroyo*. As Maud and the raiders passed, a few men raised hands to them. One called out, "*Oye*, Palo!" Another joined him, waving. Palo drew his horse close to them, pulling Maud's reins with him.

"Hey, boys, how are you?"

"Good, Palo, everybody's here. It's good to see you."

"Who's your girlfriend?"

"Not mine. Not mine. She's from a ranch. A target, I think. Got her cattle."

"Yeah, I see."

"*Generalismo* here?"

"Yeah, everybody's here."

Cervantes drew up. "Go, Palo."

"Yeah, Palo. Go," one of the campers laughed.

They rode down into the canyon around a bend. There Maud saw hundreds of people, camped for a mile down the widening stream bed. They paused for some campers who called out to the old man. Other riders drew up close to them.

"Maud. Is that you?" Maud spun around and found Ed and Frank riding toward her both on the same horse, their arms tightly drawn behind them. Maud reined her horse toward them and threw her arms around Ed. He pushed his face into her neck.

"My God. Ed. Ed." Tears filled her eyes.

"They took you! I thought you were...where's Johnnie?"

"With Maria. They made me leave him, Ed. I had to leave him."

"My God."

"What do they want with us? Isn't the cattle enough?"

"I don't know. But you're all right? They haven't hurt you?"

"Nobody touched me, but, good Lord, Ed, I don't know what to think."

"We'll get it all back, Maud. Reach in my pocket, will you." He leaned toward her.

"What?"

"Reach in my pocket. Get my tobacco bag, and roll a cigarette, will you. I'm dying."

"Lord, Ed."

She pulled a pouch out of his chest pocket, pulled a paper out of it, made a little canal in it with her forefingers, and dropped a pinch of tobacco into it. She placed it between his lips. "How about you, Frank?"

"Sure, I'll take one. Might calm me down."

"Light?"

"Top pocket."

She reached to him again and pulled out a small box of matches. She drew the match against the emery and lifted the flame to Ed's face.

"My breasts."

"What?"

"My breasts ache. Since I couldn't nurse Johnnie. They're swollen."

"Don't worry, Maud. We'll get everything back. We'll find Johnnie.

God damned thieves." Ed squinted against the smoke.

Hernandez galloped up and separated them with his blade.

"And here's another son of bitch that I need to kill." Ed rolled his shoulders to loosen his hands behind him. Frank laughed. "That's good, Ed. I want to see that."

Hernandez roared at the old man, "*Mierda antigua.* Do your fucking job, *pinches maricón.*" He smacked him across the back with his sword. The old man's horse stepped forward.

"Take care of the men, Hernandez," ordered Cervantes. "Finish the *pinche gringos.* Wait. Leave the woman."

With a nod, Hernandez checked the ropes that secured their hands behind their backs and then drove them galloping forward, the captives jerking grotesquely to stay on their saddle. He drove them into a small inlet in the canyon. Maud turned to see them off but lost sight of them as the old man directed her deeper down the trail of the canyon. Behind them a gun fired, two thin pops.

The farther they dropped into the canyon, the more congested the camp became. Every twenty yards, there was another small fire, surrounded by clusters of men. Women worked over food near tents and tarps, draped clothes over shrubs, held babies. Children darted about. A man called out, "Palo! How are you?" The old man nodded hello.

"A bride?"

The old man wagged his head and smiled. "Talk to you later."

The riders followed a turn in the ravine, a cold wind funneling against their backs. At the turn, Maud saw the remainder of the canyon, now a widened mouth opening onto a plain. The canyon floor was filled with hundreds of people, maybe a thousand, some of the camps spreading out into the mesa.

"Where are we? What is happening here?" Maud asked, looking ahead.

"This is Villa's camp. This is his army."

A group of women, some dressed in men's clothes, others in dresses, all wearing bandoliers, stared at Maud as she rode by. "Pah-low. O Pah-low"

"Good to see you, Enriqueta."

"Who's your girlfriend, Palo? She keeping your stick stiff, Palo?"

"She's not mine. Nor yours."

Maud gazed at the women, browned, haggard, angry.

"What is she for, then?"

"She's going to ride with us."

"Villa is letting a *gringa* ride with him?"

"Talk to the Colonel. I'm just keeping her company."

"Good, Palo. Hey, *gringa*. Have a good time with the stick man. Give the general our love." Enriqueta caught sight of Cervantes riding up and walked beside his horse.

"Colonel. Colonel, please, why is this *gringa* riding with you and we can't?"

"She's a target, Enriqueta. She's for the remuda. You want to take care of horses? You want to be a target"

"We want to fight."

"Well, not with me."

"Tell the *Generalísimo* that Zapata is using women."

"So is Villa."

"I mean for fighting."

"Then fight for Zapata. That's what Villa will tell you."

She waited for him to pass before she spat and returned to the other women.

The old man tugged on Maud's horse's reins, and the horse lifted its head with a start and turned away from him, snorting. He moaned and leaned off his saddle to gather up the reins again. With a hard jerk, he made Maud's horse pull alongside his. Maud looked at him for the first time. He was thick chested, short with grizzled, shaggy hair under a defeated fedora. His face was deeply wrinkled, leathery, and covered with white stubble. He felt Maud looking at him and glanced at her. His eyes were exhausted. She looked down at the horn of her saddle, then closed her eyes. He pulled the reins again, and they began to move down the ravine, passing one camp after another, each with its fire and huddled figures. Regularly, a voice would call out a greeting the old man, just as often followed by silent nods to Cervantes and Hernandez.

A reckoning was occurring to Maud, slowly and then with a terrifying urgency. She stood up in her saddle and twisted around. "Where is my husband?" The old man would not look at her but gave her horse a slight kick in its flank. It bolted ahead a length. Maud began to howl, "Ed! Ed!" People watched her from their camps. The old man made his horse skip up to her. He leaned over to her and put his arms around her small shoulders.

"*Por favor*, Señora," he whispered in her ear. "They will kill you, too."

"He's dead. That man shot him. Ed is dead."

"Yes, I think so. So, please."

Again, Hernandez drew up. "Shut your mouth, woman. Shut it or I will cut out your tongue. What are you doing, Palo? Get away from her, *pinche maricon*." He looked at him. "Palo, slap her. Slap her now and tell her, Shut up, woman." Maud faced away from him, her shoulders heaving.

Palo sat frozen. Hernandez drew his sword. "Now."

Maud turned to Hernandez. He was a thick man with a wide, blunt face, a thick nose and a square chin, covered in black stubble. He wore a khaki military shirt with epaulets. He leaned toward Palo in his saddle.

Palo opened his hand and hit Maud as lightly as he could and still make a slap. She stopped crying. She glared at him for an instant, lunged up in her stirrups, drew back her fist and punched the old man so hard his nose popped. He nearly slipped off his saddle. Blood seeped from his nostrils. He looked stunned, wide-eyed, tearing. She sat back in her saddle and slowly put her hands to her face. Hernandez laughed and rode past them.

"Palo. You are worthless. You are a worthless piece of dog shit, do you hear me? Hey, *Señora*. Don't worry about Palo. He won't hurt you. I will. I will kill you, woman, and you will be relieved when I do. I think tomorrow morning. I will check with the colonel. Let's plan on tomorrow morning."

Maud kept her hands to her face, shaking her head.

"Ed! Ed!" Hernandez laughed and rode ahead. "She's coming, Ed!"

The old man wiped blood from his lips, and they began to ride again. "I am sorry, *Señora*." Maud sat erect, keeping her eyes forward. They passed more camps, but Palo was deaf to the greetings of his friends.

Soon they were at the base of the ravine, which drained into a wide valley surrounded by mesas. Hundreds of rebels and their families were gathered in small groups. Cervantes stopped ahead of Maud and Palo, so they stopped well behind him. He was speaking to a man who held a rifle across chest. He lowered his rifle and pointed to a place around the canyon wall.

Near Palo and Maud, a group of four young men sat, one strumming a guitar.

"This is all I have so far, but I can't get the rhymes right." He cleared his throat and started sing with a thin, tremulous voice, strumming simple chords.

> Oh, young Doroteo, he saw his sister
> In the arms of the boss
> She screamed, help me brother
> And Doroteo, never at a loss
> Took his revolver and cried
> Death to land owners all
> And began to shoot
> And he's shooting still.

"Well, that doesn't rhyme. It's no good."

"That's what I mean. But that's what happened."

"*Pues, nada.* You have to change it. Villa can still shoot him. You just have to change some of the words."

"Uh huh, but if I change it, it's not so grand. He has to be, you know, continuing the struggle. It's more poetic that way, more grand. He can't just kill one man."

"He can continue the struggle in another verse, can't he? He needs to shoot just one guy at a time, like one guy each verse."

"That would be a long song. I can't write that much."

"*Pues, verdad.* Then, just one in this verse and a bunch in other ones."

"How about, Death to land owners all, and this will be the first of many, many to fall."

"Yeah, that's pretty good."

The young man with the guitar sang the new verse, and the others nodded after the line in which many fell.

Maud watched them blankly from her saddle until her horse lurched forward, following Palo's lead. They followed the path out of the ravine and into the valley. Against the canyon wall, three men stood, their arms tied behind their backs. They were stripped down to their shirts and shivered in the shadow of the stone behind them. Four men stood a short distance away from them, talking to each other and managing their rifles. Another, on horseback, raised his arm.

Palo and Maud halted their horses to stay out of range.

"Line up. Line up." The men with rifles came to a casual attention and raised their barrels. "Stand up straight," he yelled to the bound men.

"Wait! Wait!" A man rushed toward the firing squad, waving his arms. "Stop! Halt!" He was shouting in English. Another man, carrying a wooden-boxed camera and tripod on his shoulder, ran to join him. "*Espere, por favor.* He tried his Spanish to the man on horseback.

"What do you want now?"

"We need to set up the camera. *La cámara, ¿entiende?*"

A boy ran up and stood by the director and faced the captain.

"He wants you to wait for the camera."

"*Ay Dios.* We need to do some executions. Tell the *gringos* to get out of the way."

"Wait. Wait. Mr. Villa promised we could film this. Ask him. Tell him, boy, that Mr. Villa promised they could film the execution. Tell him to ask Villa. Jesus. Hurry, Carl. Let's go."

"Harry, the light's no good." The cameraman squinted through the eyepiece. "They're standing in the shade."

"How much more time till the sun lights the wall?"

"Maybe an hour."

"Tell him, boy."

"Sir, can you wait an hour to shoot the men?"

The man on horseback gritted his teeth and looked away. "Why?"

"He says they need more light. They're in the dark."

"Tell him they'll look like shadows on film. We need more light."

"He says they won't look good for the movie."

The man on horseback reined his horse in a tight circle. "We'll put them in the light. Over here in the sun."

The boy suggested this to the director and the cameraman.

"No, no. They can't stand in open space. They need to stand against a wall for contrast. Tell him, they need to be there for a better picture."

One of the bound men slumped against the rock wall. The boy turned to the man on horseback. "The movie man says they need to be by the rock to make a pretty picture when you shoot them."

The man on horseback spat and swore fiercely and at length.

"Boy, what did he say?"

"Something like he knows your mother."

"Impossible. Will he wait? Or do I need to call Mr. Villa over here? "Sir?"

The men of the firing squad were back in a circle, talking to each other. The two other bound men sat and stared at the conversation. The slumped man looked at his lap.

"An hour. No more. Men, wait an hour. Watch them. When I come back, you can shoot."

"*Muchas gracias*," offered the director, and the horseman galloped away.

Palo tugged on Maud's horse's reins and they passed by the squad, passing farther into the valley. Everywhere lay camps and fires. There were thousands of men and their families.

Ahead apace Cervantes and Hernandez rode up to a small, barrel-chested man mounted on a mule. He wore a small straw hat and a bandolier draped over each shoulder. Five men on horseback surrounded him, watching the two men approach. The man who dealt with the film director was explaining the lighting problem to the man in the straw hat. He was agreeable. "Of course we can wait. We aren't leaving for a while. Maybe noon."

"I'll tell them, then, but I think they also want to take pictures of you riding."

"*Muy bien.*"

"Wait, here he comes." The director was walking their direction, the cameraman in tow slowed by the camera and tripod on his shoulder, behind him, the boy translator.

"Greetings, General!" The director smiled broadly. Villa nodded, lifting his hat a bit. The horsemen drew nearer to his mule as he leaned forward in his saddle.

"*¿Qué es lo que necesita de nosotros esta mañana,* Harry?"

"A delay, sir, on the execution until…"

"Yes, I know that. That can wait an hour. Anything else?"

"I want to shoot you riding."

"*Quiere tomar fotos de usted montando su caballo.*"

"E-shoot me? Why e-shoot me?"

"Film you."

"Ah. *¿Esta mañana?*"

"If possible."

"*Bueno. Vamos a hacerlo ahora.*"

"Good, except…we need you to get dressed."

"I am fully clothed."

"Your hat, General. We need you to wear something serious."

"A serious hat?"

"Your general's hat, with a badge on it. The straw hat doesn't look good for a battle. It's not serious enough."

Villa waved Cervantes and Hernandez to come closer. "The movie man doesn't like my hat. *¿Qué piensan? ¿No es bastante serio?*"

"You are serious, sir, no matter the hat."

"Yes, but, really, can you take orders from a head wearing this thing?"

Cervantes peered at it. "It's true, it's not a general's hat. It's more like a farmer's hat."

"I do have my general hat here. I'll put it on."

"And your uniform, sir."

Villa looked at him.

"Sir, *Generalísimo*, the studio went to great expense to have these uniforms made. Could you wear one? It makes you look more like a general."

"*Más serio.*"

"Exactly, sir."

"My men don't like them. They say they're uncomfortable for riding."

"The trousers?"

"They say the pants squeeze their balls when they ride. Isn't that true, Cervantes?"

The director looked to Cervantes.

"They feel tight. I don't like them. But they look nice, it's true."

"Well, you understand, don't you? I can't lead men into battles when their balls are turning blue. They'll be...distracted."

"Well, how about the shirts? Do they like the shirts?"

"Pretty much. Cervantes, you're wearing one, aren't you?"

Cervantes nodded and patted his chest.

"Can you wear one for the camera, General?"

"So I can look like Cervantes? Anything!"

"And tell your men to wear them, at least when we're shooting."

"To look serious."

"Yes."

Villa turned to the guards near him. "Well, you heard the boss. Put on your shirts and get serious." The guards looked at one another. "*Ahorita.*"

Two rode off to their camps. One stepped off his horse and walked to a nearby camp. He shouted at a woman, who ducked into a tent.

"Will we be riding with you to shoot your next raid?"

"No, it's too far away. And it's a secret. You would probably be killed."

"All right, then. Can we get some battle scenes from you this morning?"

"Here?"

"When the sun is higher up."

"Who would I shoot?"

"You don't need to kill anyone. Just shoot around a little bit while you ride."

"But who would be shooting at me?"

"Nobody. We'll make it look like there's an army attacking you." Villa nodded.

"So, General, we'll see you in an hour, here, in your uniform."

Turning from the director, Villa spoke to his men. "Well, Cervantes, what do you have for us? What happened?"

"We finished a few raids and got a couple hundred head." He turned around in his saddle until he spotted Maud and Palo. "And we got this woman, a horsewoman, I think. Thought we could use her during the raid."

Noticing Villa's attention, Palo tugged on Maud's horse's reins and they rode to his superiors. "General," he nodded to Villa.

"Good day, Palo! Who's your friend?"

"Her name is Maud." Maud's eyes widened. She glared at Villa.

"*Señor* Villa, why have you...?"

Villa put his hand up. "If you have something to say, say it to my colonels. That's what they are here for."

"These men took my baby from me. They killed my husband. Did you kill my husband?" She looked at Hernandez.

Hernandez raised his eyebrows to Villa, nodding.

"Well," Villa said. "It can't be helped. Good job, men."

"Should we just kill her now?" Cervantes asked. "*Yo no la quiero.*"

"No, we'll take her with us. Can you take care of horses? If you can, you can live for a few more days. If you can't, Cervantes wants to kill you. I don't know why."

"I know horses."

"Right, then, she'll attend the remuda during the raid. Her Spanish is good, isn't it. Strange but good. Cervantes, put a guard on her, take care of her. No need to kill her—unless she becomes a problem. The ride to the raid will probably do her in, anyway."

"What raid?"

Villa put his hand up again to Maud. "Cervantes, we've got about four hundred, including your men. We'll leave at twilight. Now, I have some business." He smiled broadly, reined his mule away from them and rode up the canyon. His guards followed him.

Sunlight was dropping down the rock walls and the day was warming. The air smelled of wood smoke.

"We'll rest here. Palo, watch her. I need to sleep."

They dismounted. Maud loosened the cinch of her horse's saddle, dropped the saddle in the shade, and tied the mule's reins loosely to a shrub.

"*¿Señora, quiere un poco de comida?*"

Maud shook her head. She lay down, resting her head on her saddle, and began to dream.

She woke to gunshot, jerking herself upright. Nearby, a row of men were lowering their rifles amid gun smoke. Men with their hands tied behind them slid lankly against the rock wall, spilling to the ground. The man with the camera moved followed their motion downward, slowly working the crank on the side of the box.

"Cut, cut. Light's perfect. Let's get Villa out here." The director shaded his eyes. "Can someone find Villa. Tell him we're ready."

Maud's eyes ached, and her chest cramped with a rush of memories from the night before. She cupped her forehead, pressing the butt of her hands against her eyes, and rested her elbows on her knees. Immediately, she fell asleep. Again, she woke to gun fire.

"Again, again, but slower. Tell him, ride by slower. *Más despacio, más lento.* Where's the translator?"

Villa was mounted on a beautiful black charger, its saddle black with a silver horn. He wore a general's hat and military garb, and he held a pistol in each hand.

"General, that was perfect, but you have to do everything slower. Ride by the camera slower. All we'll get is a blur. Somebody tell him what a blur is. Slow, sir. *Mas depascio, por favor. Lento!*" Villa nodded at him and turned his horse around.

"Action. Go, ride. Ride." Villa trotted his horse by the camera, shooting his pistols in the air.

"Jesus. This is impossible. All right. Let's try it again but focus on him, not so much of his horse."

A crowd had gathered in a semicircle around the scene. "Get back. Get them back, please. Away from the *General*."

A woman called out. "Please, *General*, could you not shoot at us? *Usted nos está haciendo poniendo nerviosos*."

Villa turned to the crowd. "I'm shooting at the walls. Not at you."

"Yes, of course. But sometimes, you know, the bullets go everywhere. You know we don't have magic like you."

"*No te preocupes*. Nobody dies here unless the movie man likes the light."

The director shouted. "Again. All right, ride by." Villa nudged his charger. "That's right, now shoot. *Pistolos!* Shoot! Right! Grimace. Grimace at the camera, like you want to kill it. Shoot, keep shooting!"

Villa stopped and turned his horse again and waited for directions.

"Tell him, all right, tell him, ride slower. And grimace at the camera. Do you know 'grimace'?"

The translator shook his head.

"Grimace. Like fierce. Like this." He stretched his lips over his teeth.

"*Generale*, he wants you to look like this." He turned to the director. "Can you do that again?"

The director grimaced at Villa.

"He wants you to look like that. *Lo siento*."

Villa laughed. "He looks like he needs to shit.

"And tell him, point a gun at the camera and grimace."

"He wants you to get angry at the camera, like you want to shoot it."

"*Muy fácil.*"

"All right, again. Action!"

Villa rode toward the camera slowly, shooting over heads, turning his as if he had heard shots from behind, and shooting again. When he neared the camera, he snarled into the lens and shot into the tripod'ss legs, and then rode on, shooting at the sky.

The cameraman blanched and stepped back from the tripod and held up his palms. "I think I'm done with this, Harry."

"Yeah, that's right. I think we got what we needed." He turned to Villa, "Thank you, General. That was *muy perfecto*. You'll be in the news all across America very, very soon."

The translator passed the word, and Villa nodded. "*Verdad. Eso es cierto.*"

At twilight the old man shook Maud a little on her shoulder. She awoke in terror and then closed her eyes. "It's time to go, *Señora.*" The air was already cold. Nearby, men passed silently on horseback, riding out of the canyon. Overhead, bats swooped in short, jerky arches between the walls of the canyon.

Maud pulled the serape down over her head. Her face was tender, burnt from sleeping in the sun. She saddled her mare and mounted. When Palo was ready, they joined the column of men.

They reached the mouth of the canyon where hundreds of men, all on horseback, had gathered. Villa and his guards rode along the outside of the group, Villa shouting orders. He found Palo and Maud. "Take her to the front of the line." The old man nodded, and taking Maud's reins, he trotted their horses to the head of the procession. With a shout from Villa, repeated by his colonels down the line, the column rode out to the darkening mesa.

MARCH 3

What if he says no?
Well, you've got a horse, don't you?
You know I do.
Then use it.

The night was cold, moonless and starlit. They rode for hours, taking odd, circuitous routes, spending little time on mesas, resorting to mountain paths. Maud led the column, mutely, directed quietly by Palo.

"*Señora, lo siento por todo.*"

Maud didn't respond.

"*Señora?*"

"If you're so sorry..." She stopped.

"I can't help you. *¿Me entiende?*"

"Then there's nothing to say. Don't tell me sorry." She raised her voice.

"*No me entiende, Señora.* You don't know." He grew silent. "He would kill me if I help you escape."

"Who?"

"Villa. Cervantes. Hernandez. They would kill me in a moment if they saw you were gone."

"What's so important about me?"

"It's not that. They will kill me if I make a mistake. Another mistake and I'm dead." They rode silently for a few minutes.

"We all are afraid. We fear Villa more than we fear Carranza. If we give him a reason, we would be like the men you saw this morning, waiting to be shot. Some of these men are from Cervante's home town, Namiquipa, south of you. He forced them to come with him. Said he'd shoot them, otherwise. Or kill their families if they ran away. So, you know."

"I thought you people love Villa."

"The people in the camp love him. His guards, the *Dorados*, too. For those of us who fight with him, it's hard to say love. But I know for certain I fear him. He is a very hard man. *No quiero morir todavia*."

"I don't want to die yet either, but I didn't volunteer for this."

"You're a *gringa*. You signed up when you moved to Mexico."

"What good is this?" Maud whispered. "Why take me, why kill my husband?

Palo was silent.

"Why put me up front here?"

"Caranza's men. If they see us, they'd probably see you first, huh?"

"So?"

"Maybe they won't shoot a woman. They'd see your dress, your hair."

"You don't think they'd shoot me?"

"Well, if they did, it wouldn't be a problem for us. *Lo siento*. That's what Villa would say."

Maud turned away from Palo. "I don't much care for this talk." Palo saw her rub her eyes and reached to pat her shoulder. Two charred balls of beef hung from the horn of his saddle. He untied one and passed it to Maud. "*Bueno. Come ésta.*"

They rode in a dark silence. Maud put the meat to her mouth. It was burnt and dusty. She bit into it and gagged. It was raw inside. She brushed away some of the dirt and bit into the cooked shell, then tied it to her saddle.

Maud's horse followed the trail as she drifted into a chaotic dream, filled with wrestling, struggling figures.

What if he says no?

Then he says no.

Will you marry me anyway?

I told you, you got a horse, so use it.

At dawn word came up from the back of the line line, stop for a rest. The riders dismounted along the path and rested by their horses. Maud pulled the saddle and blanket off her horse and dropped it away from the path. Frank's saddle, Frank's horse. She glanced back to look for anyone riding Ed's. Nothing. She lay down, using the saddle seat to rest her head. She pulled her *serape* tighter against the chill of the ground and closed her eyes. Palo sat nearby.

She heard some riders approach the front of the file. Villa spoke in a pressured whisper.

"We'll be rich, you know. The money is there, waiting for us."

"Also the army."

"I've got reports. The army is weak. Juan, tell them what you saw."

"There are hundreds of soldiers in a garrison."

"See."

"But their arms are not available to them so easily. They keep them locked up."

"This is why we need to surprise them," said Villa. "If we surprise them in the morning, they'll just stand up to get shot. Which, of course, we will do." He laughed. The others laughed.

"Then we'll get their arms and break open the banks."

"When?"

"Soon. We'll stay in the hills a while, keep moving around so the *federales* aren't aware. Then we'll cross the plain to Columbus. What does it look like for the attack?"

Juan moved his boot across the dirt. "There's a hill outside of the town that will hide us. Then closer, there's an *arroyo* along the town, along the train tracks. We can surprise them from there."

"It's a small town. Why there? Why not some place big? El Paso?"

"Guns. The US Army will arm us. And another thing. Remember Sam Ravel, the gun man?"

"He robbed us."

Maud recognized Cervantes' voice.

"That's right. He took our money but kept the guns. He lives in Columbus. He owns a hotel. Did you see it, Juan?"

"The Commercial Hotel. His wife and son live there too."

"Another reason to attack Columbus. We will burn it to the ground. We will kill Ravel."

Maud kept her eyes closed. Frank's horse was fast, she remembered, and it didn't seem that tired. The conference of men drifted off. She heard Villa from a distance, shouting and laughing. He was riding his smaller mount, a sorrel mule.

All along the path, men were lying down resting. Palo was nearby. He propped himself up and reached to Maud with a canteen. "*¿Quiere un poco de agua, señora?*"

"*No.*"

"*Tiene que tomar agua.*"

"Help yourself."

The old man dropped his head against a folded *serape* and began to breathe deeply.

Maud waited till she heard the sound of snoring. The sun was now over the mountain ridge, lighting the valley with golden shafts, and the air was warming. She stood and lifted her saddle and blanket slowly, noiselessly and slid it over the back of her horse. It shivered and snorted, taking a step forward. She shushed it and patted its shoulder. She reached beneath its chest to hold the saddle's cinch strap rings still and fed the lash through them. She gave the cinch an extra tug, took the reins and led the horse a little farther down the path. She heard a voice behind her in the distance and a shout. She slipped her foot into the stirrup, swung her leg over the horse's back and snapped the reins in a single movement. The horse bolted down the path, and Maud, her knees pressed against the horse's ribs, flattened her back parallel to the horse's spine. "Het, het," she swatted the horse's flank, and it raced down the rocky path.

Two *Dorados* were already mounted and riding in pursuit, firing at Maud. The path, rocky and steep, slowed Maud's horse. She forced it to jump stony wash where a rivulet had taken out the path, but beneath it the path took an abrupt turn. The footing felt uncertain, and the horse reeled sidewise, whinnying, and reared up. Maud stood in the stirrups, "Easy, easy!" The horse calmed down but stood still. A bullet slapped a nearby rock.

Maud reined the horse around and rode it back up the path. She passed the *Dorados* without looking at them. They followed her back to the company. One kept his rifle out. Villa met them on the path.

"*¿Quieres morir?*"

"*Pues. ¿Por qué no?* You're going to kill me. Why don't you just kill me now?"

"I'll tell you something. Listen to me now. This ride will be very hard. Some of my men will die on their saddles. I do not think you can live through this. But if you don't die from the ride, I will not kill you. No one will hurt you. And if you live, I set you free."

"Set me free?"

"If you live."

"Set me free now."

"If you live."

"Cervantes will kill me."

"Maybe. I will tell the men to leave you alone, including him."

Maud nodded. "And Hernandez."

"Let's go back. We have a mule for you to ride now."

"I like mules fine."

"So do I. This is a very slow mule. Especially for you."

Palo stood shamefaced. Cervantes was on horseback near him.

"Cervantes, take her horse and give the mule. Palo, do you know how to tie a knot?"

"Of course, *Generalísimo*."

"Practice on *Señora* Maud. Tie her and keep her tied."

They rode through the day, staying close to the mountains, silently following the path along the range's base. In the late afternoon, there was a yell from the rear, and the order was passed to the front of the line. The riders shifted off their horses and made camp along the flat of a canyon.

Farther up the *arroyo* was the ruin of an adobe house, walls and a door. Cervantes directed Palo to lead Maud into the house. Within the walls, Maud lifted her tied wrists to the old man. "Please. No need for this if I am in jail."

Palo looked over his shoulder and then untied her. "Lie down, sleep for a while."

"And will you take the saddle off the mule? He will need rest too."

"*Sí, por supuesto, Señora.*" Palo left the house.

Cervantes cried out to some nearby riders, "Boys, before you rest, pile your saddles here at the door. Aquí," he pointed. Men wearily lugged their saddles and dropped them in front of the house, and soon the door was blocked by a chest-high stack, nearly as wide as the house.

Palo returned to the door and spoke over the pile. "*Señora, ¿quiere un traguito de agua?*" He set her canteen on the seat of the top saddle. "There is still a little in here."

"*Sí, gracias,* Palo." Maud took the canteen.

He smiled at her over the saddles. "And would you like your meat?"

Maud frowned. "Leave it on the saddle." She found a patch of sunlight on the ground and lay down to rest.

If he says no, then off we go.
If he says no, then off we go.
Sneak off? Just like that?
Well, you don't want to stay around here when he finds out.
True.
He would break you in two.
Hey now, don't be so. I can fight. You might be surprised.
You better not fight my daddy, or I'd have to kill you, too. So would my brothers.
Good, but after you all killed me, we'd still be married.
Yeah, that might slow them down a little. Me being a widow.
I don't care. They can kill me. You can kill me. It's worth it.
That's nice.
But still, all considered, I like sneaking off better than the getting killed part.
Uh huh.
If he says no.

Oh, he'll say no all right.
You're so sure?
He don't want me leaving, I'm double sure of that.
Then off we go.
To where? You have an idea.
El Paso, I reckon. I can work there.
Maud slept a while and woke in the dark, thinking hard.

MARCH 4

Maud lay on the dirt floor of the house, thinking, looking at stars through the log rafters of the adobe. She thought about escape, wished for weapons, and imagined saving the people of Columbus from the raid. Her breasts ached, swollen with milk, and were seeping into the front of her dress. She stood at the door and peered through the saddles. Men lay nearby, some with their heads toward the door and their feet toward a fire. Beyond the glow of the fire, the ground was blue white with frost. Beyond the firelight, she could see a black horse tied to a shrub close to the trail. She listened for the men's snoring.

The fire popped. She listened and heard no movement. Very slowly, she pulled the top saddle off the stack and set it lightly down inside the wall. She listened, and then picked up another saddle, lifting it high to keep the cinch rings from hitting the saddle below it. She set it down gingerly.

She could now see easily out the door. The horse was about fifty feet away. It was the sleek charger Villa rode for the filming. The fire popped and sizzled, but the snoring remained rhythmic. She lifted another saddle.

Soon she had lowered the pile to a height a little lower than her waist. She leaned out the door to size up the camp. She hiked up her dress and held it in her fist. She raised a leg and slid it over the top saddle on the pile and sat for a moment, listening. Satisfied, she rolled the rest of the way over the pile. Her boot touched the ground immediately next to Palo's ear. Her dress hem folded over his forehead.

She jerked her dress up and stood still. The fire crackled. Palo puffed air from his mouth and rolled to his side. Maud stepped lightly and quickly over several sleeping men until she reached the black horse. It snorted, and Maud ducked behind its body. After a moment, she patted its shoulder, sounding a light shush, shush. The horse stiffened and stepped sideways. Maud stepped slightly back until it calmed itself. The horse arched its neck to look at her.

It had gotten itself tangled up in its reins. A rope was tied to the reins to reach the shrub, and the horse had gotten it wrapped around its foreleg, making it skittish. Maud kneeled down and tried to lift the foreleg to unravel the rope, but the horse stamped its hoof and whinnied. Again, Maud stepped back and hid in the horse's shadow and listened. She began to untie the rope from the shrub instead, but she heard a scuffle and saw a pair of legs on the other side horse. She slowly raised herself until, looking over the shoulders of the horse, she recognized Palo, his face a shadow against the fire.

"What are you doing here?" she hissed.

Palo looked drowsy and baffled.

"And you?" he managed.

"Villa's horse. It's tangled up. Help me get him loose. Quietly."

Palo knelt and lifted the horse's foreleg while Maud slipped the rope over its hoof.

He whispered, "Go back to the house. Don't wake anyone."

Maud patted the horse.

"*Váyase, ahora,*" he mouthed. He raised his thick eyebrows.

Maud saw his rifle. She had nothing. Her mind raced as she stood.

Palo stepped around the horse and took her by hand. "Come." He held his rifle up a bit. Maud let him lead her hand in hand. Then as if awakening, she tore her hand from his, her face contorted with sorrow.

Palo watched her delicately step over the sleeping men, her dress hem raised, and return to the house. Once inside the house, she quietly lifted the saddles, one after another, back in place. Her skin was bright from the fire. As he stood guard, she disappeared behind the stack.

At dawn Maud was awakened by the sound of the men pulling their saddles from her door. Palo was peering into the hut. She lifted her canteen, shook it and listened for water. She emptied it with a swallow and pulled its strap over her shoulder. She left the hut, giving Palo a long, level stare. The men were nearly all mounted when she lifted her saddle to her mule's back. Once she was mounted, Palo showed her the lash. She put her wrists together to be tied.

They rode higher into the mountains, following a narrow trail. The rock and pine were blue with dawn, frost clung to the gravel and small plants and a chilling breeze slid off the mountain. The men were utterly silent. Many slept in their saddles, their shoulders slumped forward, their heads nodding slowly to the rhythm of their horses' steps.

They reached a pass open to the sun. From behind men shouted forward the order to stop. Maud relaxed her shoulders against the warmth and looked at the valley below. In the distance a solitary figure, barely visible, ran across the desert. Palo lifted his chin in the direction of the runner. "Rarámuri. A Tarahumarah Indian. Maybe a messenger. He might be telling his people about us."

"He is running a long way," Maud said.

"He will run all day."

"I feel like I could do that."

Palo nodded at her. Nearby Villa was talking to his captains who had circled their horses around him. He was crowned with his straw hat and was riding a small sorrel mule. He was talking excitedly, pointing to the horizon to the northwest, the captains nodding. Cervantes pulled away from the circle and rode to Palo.

"How is you girlfriend, Palo? You keeping her tied down?"

"She is tied."

Hernandez joined them.

"When do we kill her?"

"I thought today. Maybe tomorrow."

"Villa promised me that you would leave me alone."

"I did not hear that. I will make sure to get his permission before we shoot you."

"As far as I care, you could do it right here, right now. Save me from having to look at you."

"The *gringa* is sad today. Maybe we can put you out of your misery. Palo, get moving down that goat trail. We're heading for the Padilla ranch for this evening."

Palo reined his horse toward the trail, using his right hand to prompt Maud's mule down a long sloping trail into the valley below.

Why do you think he doesn't like me?

You're older than he'd like.

Too old for you?

Maybe. Ten years, right? Maybe it's because you're foreign.

British? That's not so foreign.

Well, the way you talk, that's pretty foreign. He said something about that.

Maybe he just doesn't want to give you up.

Just as likely.

Well, what if he says no?

You have a horse, don't you? I have one, too.

I remember the first time I saw you.

Uh huh.

In Oklahoma.

Yeah.

And your old man had just hired me. He told me, Go uphill and help the girl.

He called me the girl?

Yes. So I rode uphill thinking you'd be picking flowers or something delicate. But you were wrestling with that team of mules.

Not unusual. I remember that day. I saw you.

You scared the life out of me. I'd never seen a tougher woman.

Well, they were mules.

You won. I sat in my saddle and watched.

Thank you for the help.

You were jerking those reins around, and the mules looked like they'd do anything just to please you.

I got them moving, it's true.

And they dragged that chain load of logs down that hill, all the while you're yelling at them. If they hadn't been tethered, I think they'd have fled in terror.

Fled. See. That's British.

Ah. So when I talk to your father, I shouldn't say flee. Like, Good sir, if you don't give me your daughter's hand, we will flee forthwith.

Yeah, don't say that.

I'll say, Fella, if you'll don't say yup, we'll get some dust up.

Well, then he'd shoot you, but I reckon at least he'd understand you.

All right. Then get your horse ready. Will you bring much?

Just a handle.

You didn't act like you noticed me that day.

Maybe I noticed you were sitting on your bottom while I was breaking my back over a load of logs. In a dress.

Yes, you were a sight. Sweating, yelling, your hair all fallen in your face. Very attractive.

Must have been glorious.

Maud's canteen was empty. Her tongue was thick and dry.

"Is there any water?"

Palo shook his head. His eyes were glazed, his eyelids heavy.

"Can we get some?"

"There's no water."

Maud turned her mule around and looked at the line of men behind her. They were quiet, and most were slumped in their saddles, rocking with the steps of their mounts.

"We haven't had any water for two days."

"You gave me some last night."

"That was the last of mine."

She turned her mule back to the trail.

"There might be some down below."

"At the ranch?"

"Yes, that is what we think. And some cattle."

There was some shouting from behind. Maud stopped again and turned around. A rider had fallen from his horse. A captain rode up to him and ordered him back on his saddle. The man looked up at him but stayed prone. The captain lifted his rifle from his saddle holster and tilted the barrel toward the fallen rider. The rider stood and threw both arms over his saddle to hold himself erect. Then he raised himself up on his stirrup and sat in his saddle. The captain motioned toward Palo, and the line began to move again.

It was later though, you know.
What?
When I fell for you.
When?
You were on one of your father's racehorses out on the paddock.
Paddock?
Field. You were running that horse at top speed. You were up off the saddle. You were leaning forward like a jockey, riding faster than anybody I'd ever seen. Much less a woman. That got to me.
My pa says I ride better than my brothers.
There's no doubt. Do they say that?
They don't talk about it. It's true that I can handle a horse.
How about your brothers?
What?
Can you handle them?
I had to teach them some lessons when they were younger. Now they know how to act toward me.
I guess I'm in for some lessons?
Probably. I'll go easy on you.
Try.

By twilight they reached the ranch. Maud pulled aside and watched some captains approach the house. They shouted some greetings, but there was not answer. Cervantes walked to the front door. It was half open, so he pushed it open and walked in. After a moment, he came back out. Villa had arrived, and Cervantes shook his head at him.

"*No hay nada aquí.*"

Without waiting for orders, some riders headed for a water tank. They brushed aside the algae that bunched by the edge of the tank and brought handfuls of water to their faces. Others came and drank and filled their canteens.

Some riders fanned out into a nearby field and rounded up a couple dozen head of cattle into a corral. One by one, they roped them by the horns and pulled them to a couple of men who sliced their throats and drained their blood. Others pulled knives and began slicing off the skin and digging into bone joints.

Palo and Maud dismounted, tying their animals to a shrub. The horse and mule bowed their heads immediately, chewing on clumps of withered grass. Palo led Maud by the lash the bound her wrists, taking her to where some men were breaking up a span of fence for firewood. They made several pyres, and once they had skinned and severed chunks of beef, the butchers piled it on the fire.

The sun had gone down. The sky was black blue with a sliver of a moon. The flames leaped as the meat sizzled and burned. Cooks pulled the charred beef off the fire and hung it off a nearby branch. As it cooled, men stepped up and sliced off pieces the size of a doubled fist. The insides were raw, oozing blood.

Maud lay down a distance from one of the fires and watched while the men gnawed on the meat. When the fires were reduced to orange coals, Villa walked from group to group, cheering the men on, patting their backs and laughing. He placed himself near one of the fires and called out for attention.

"*Escúchenme, escúchenme, mis amigos.*" The crowd grew still. "We are about to do something for the history books. In a few more days, no more, we will begin the invasion of North America. We will start with one town. But from that town, on we go to great things. Even as we gather, this little army, to reach into the United States, other forces are mobilizing to come to our assistance. They are waiting for us to begin the action, and when we invade, they will invade."

The men were rapt. They gazed at him with astonishment, their faces gilt by the glow of the coals.

"*¿Quiénes son esos amigos?* Even now, men, our allies, Japan and Germany, are waiting for this historic moment. This invasion is their signal, a sign for them to engage in this conquest. *Sí, es verdad.* I have received their assurance. We come from the south, like a sword thrust, and then the Japanese and German forces will come from west and east. Together we will squeeze the life out of these monsters to the north."

Men cheered, whooping and clapping.

"Do you know when I arrived at this plan? What was the moment that changed the direction of my thinking? Perhaps you think, isn't it enough to fight Carranza? To continue our struggle with our brothers to the south to rid ourselves of this illness? But where does Carranza get his power, his money, his arms? The United States, *hermanos.*

"They took our land to the north, and now we see them moving into Mexico, little by little, stealing our land, our minerals. We will fight with our lives to protect our country and return it to its former glory. *¡Ustedes, todos ustedes deben hacer esto!*"

Villa put his palms out toward his men and patted the air to quiet them. "*Escúchenme, ahora. Escuchen todos a mi sueño.* In this great endeavor, this terrible act of justice, you will be rewarded. Not only by the act of justice but by riches you cannot imagine. Do you want to be rich?"

Some men cheered.

"You have only to reach out and take what you want in North America. When we defeat this town, you will see the beginning of your wealth. From town to town, from city to city, you will take what you want, what should have been yours all along. Wealth the *gringos* stole from us, we will return to Mexican hands. Your hands, my friends."

More cheering and laughter.

"Are you tired from our travels today, from this long journey, from our years of fighting? Take heart. *Sé fuerte.* Find your strength now. We are looking to the north to change Mexico forever. There is no room for fatigue, only the rage for justice. When we come to Columbus, we will kill every gringo we see. They will run in terror. And we will use them as torches, burning them as they made living torches of our friends. Terror! And that terror will spread before us, as cities lay open to our invasion!"

Men got to their feet, cheering, howling and shooting at the night sky. Maud worked at the leather that lashed her wrists together but could not loosen it.

MARCH 5

"Señora. Señora, despiértese."

Maud could not wake in the black of the night. She opened her eyes, closed them and slept immediately. Palo jostled her shoulder. *"Señora, es hora de salir."* He took a slab of the meat they had cooked and placed it under her nose. "Wake up. Eat something quickly. We have to go."

The smell of the meat made Maud retch. She woke, wild eyed, jerking herself away from Palo, her lashed hands covering her mouth. "Is that my husband? Is that my husband? You cooked my husband?" She gagged and coughed at the ground.

"Señora Maud. You have to eat or you will be sick."

Maud sat up, sullen, her hand to her mouth.

"We have to travel now at night. There are *federales*, we think. We need to move back up to the mountains. There is water in your canteen."

The air was cold, the sky starlit with a sliver of moon. The riders saddled their horses wordlessly by the glow of the embers. When they were mounted, fist-sized hunks of meat tied to their saddle horns, Palo and Maud rode to the front of the troop and led them away from the ranch.

If it's a boy, Johnnie.
Fine with me. You don't want to name him after your father?
Not really, except it might calm him a bit.

Well, Johnnie's fine. How much longer?
A couple of weeks, I reckon.
And if it's a girl?
Johnnie.
Pretty soon, we need to get back down to Pearson.
The ranch?
Yeah, things have quieted down. From what I hear.
That's good.

The night air bit at Maud. She bunched her shoulders under her *serape*, keeping her elbows close to her body. Certain that the action wouldn't be noticed, she stroked her breasts to express some milk. Then, exhausted, she drifted in and out of sleep. The path was wide, and a couple of riders joined Palo.

"Palo, will you stay in the north after we take it?" a rider asked.

"I still have family in Sonora. I'll go back there."

"How long have you known the General?"

"Years. I was with him when he rode with Carranza."

"He never gets hurt, does he."

"Not yet."

"Somebody told me he was blessed by a priest and can't get killed."

"It's a special vest," the other rider chimed in. "That's what I heard. Something invisible."

"I don't think so," Palo said. "I think he's just careful."

"True. He has the guards."

"Yes, the guards. And he's always watching."

"My family, we all love him. *A ti también, Palo, ¿no?*"

"Of course. I would give him my life. I probably will."

"Did you see them kill that guy yesterday?"

"*¿Qué tipo?*"

"The one, he fell off his saddle. They told him, get back up, but he was dazed."

"They killed him?"

"Yeah, they told him, get up or die, like that."

"So, he didn't get back on his horse?"

"No, he just sat there on the ground, staring at them. Two *Dorados* pulled him off the trail and stabbed him, just like that."

"I didn't hear anything."

"It was at the back of the column. What do you think about that?"

"The men are staying on their horses now, *supongo*."

"Yeah, but I think this guy, he was just too tired. And thirsty. So he couldn't do anything but sit."

Palo nodded. "Well, let's stay on our saddles, right? For Villa. For the revolution."

The two riders slowed and let Palo pass ahead of them.

Maud looked at him. "What was that?"

"An interrogation, I think."

"Aren't they your friends?"

"Everyone is Villa's friend first."

They rode for a while in silence.

"*Necesito tener mi bebé.* I want my baby. When this is over."

Palo nodded.

When Maud woke again, it was still dark. "They call you Paulo?"

"Palo"

"Palo, like a stick? Wood?"

"Something like that."

"Is that your name?"

"No. It's a nickname, *un apodo*."

"Palo? How did you get it?"

"I can't really explain it to you."

"*Entiendo bien el español. Ya lo sabes.*"

"I can't tell you because you're a woman."

The moon, a sliver, hung on the west, and the sky sparkled with stars. Maud's face stung in the cold. She put her hands to her cheeks, and they hurt to the touch.

"You thought we cooked your husband. Back there."

"I was asleep." After a few minutes, "Anyway, why wouldn't you?"

"We aren't cannibals. We're fighting a war."

"Against me?"

"*No. Sí, en parte.*"

"What did I ever do to you? What did Ed ever do to you?"

"You're here. *México es para nosotros, no es de ustedes.*"

"We bought that ranch, fair and square."

"You bought it. That is true. But what is fair, Villa decides."

The rode for a while in silence.

"*Quiero verle a mi bebé.*"

"*Por supuesto.*"

Maud went quiet again, then nodded back to sleep.

Can we go back?

Do you want to?

You think it's safe? I don't want to go back for more trouble.

At sunup Maud awoke in her saddle to the sound of raiders racing ahead of her. The column had descended from the mountain trail, and as they reached the plain, the riders, two dozen of them, peeled away from the column to the left. Another squad galloped to the right. Ahead of them, Maud saw the ranch house they had scouted from the mountain pass. About fifty head of cattle were grazing in the distance, some lifting their heads to watch the raiders.

The middle column approached the house slowly, passing through a gate of wires strung between two posts. Cervantes galloped to the front of the column. The flanks began shouting and whistling as they rounded the cattle toward the center of the ranch. A black man stepped out the small adobe house, wearing long johns and overalls. "What the good goddamn is going on here?" He shouted in English and ran toward the fields. He spun around and shouted at Cervantes.

"*¿Qué están haciendo?* Hey, hey." He waved his arms to the riders in the field.

A Mexican woman and two dark children came to the door. The man rubbed his face and turned to Cervantes. "*¿Y ahora qué? ¡Qué carajo!*"

Cervantes spoke cooly to him. "We were wondering what food you could offer us." Maud and Palo rode away a bit from the column, now bunching in front of the house. Villa reined his horse forward and joined Cervantes. He introduced himself.

"*¿Cómo se llama?*"

"Buck Spencer."

"Buck? Is that a name?"

"Edwin."

"*Señor* Buck, from America, I guess."

"I live here now. This is my family."

"*Sí, ya veo.*" Villa dismounted and waved to Cervantes to join him.

"What kind of food do you have, Buck?" They walked to the door of the house.

That night they roasted corn and slaughtered and roasted a few head of cattle. Then they ladled streams of molasses into their mouths. The raiders roped Buck's wrists together and sat him next to Maud. She was chewing a little on an ear of corn.

He looked at her wrists. *¿Por qué estás atado?*

"Same as you. American."

"You ain't American. I reckoned you for one of them."

"How's that?"

"You wearing Mexican clothes for one thing." Buck twisted his face, then watched the fire for a while. "And your face is all red. You're like some kind of Indian or something."

"My face is red?"

"Sure enough. You been in the sun too long, I guess."

"I been in everything too long." Maud patted her sore face.

"No offense, but you stink like sour milk. And your hair, I don't know. You're pretty dirtied up, sorry to say it.

"Figures. I've been with them for some days now. Can barely make out how many."

"Well, what are you riding with them for? You got a ring. Where's your man?

"Dead, I think. They...these hooligans. They did us the same dirt like they're doing you. And they took me. They already ate up my cattle."

"Couldn't get away?"

"Tried a couple of times. No luck."

"Well, hell, they ain't gonna take me. I'd start shooting before I let that happen."

"Uh huh. Well, go on. Get shootin'." She raised her wrists to him.

"We'll see, that's all."

"Lookin' forward to it. Been wishing for somebody to do some shooting, except not at me. Had some of that. Thanks for the corn."

"Yeah, my goddamn pleasure. These fellows going to ruin me for the year, I guess."

Men began to saddle their horses. Cervantes brought Palo over to Maud and Buck. "Now you have two of them. Buck, there is your horse."

"Now wait just a moment. Wait. I am not going anywhere."

"You can stay and get shot. Maybe your wife, too."

"No, no, don't. Don't do that."

"Then get on the horse."

Buck ran to his house, his hands folded in front of him. "Elena. Elena." Cervantes drew his pistol and shot at the ground beside him. Buck stopped short, but Elena had come out of the house. He shouted to her. "They are taking me. Stay inside. Keep the children." Elena hurried back into the dark of the house.

The day warmed as the sun climbed. The raiders rode northeasterly, skirting the edge of the foothills. A few men drove Buck's cattle behind the column, raising a cloud of dust. Palo rode a little behind Buck and Maud.

"Where are we going?"

"You won't believe it. I scarcely can."

Buck looked at Maud.

"We're attacking America."

Buck snorted.

"Seriously."

"Well, I'll be. Where? The Alamo, I bet."

"Naw, just up north here. Columbus."

"Columbus! Why the hell, who wants that?"

"Villa. He's starting small."

"And shitty."

"Then the Germans and Japanese are coming."

"They want Columbus, too?"

"No. Everything. All of America, as far as I can figure. Villa has it all worked out in his mind."

Buck turned in his saddle, surveying the column of riders. When his horse slowed, Palo prodded Buck with the barrel of his rifle.

"You need to leave me alone, fellow."

"He don't speak English."

"Just as goddamned well."

They rode in silence.

"What's his name?"

"The old guy? Palo."

"He needs to leave me alone."

"Tell him yourself."

"I just might. I just might."

"He's been good enough to me. Keeps me in water."

"Hey, Paulo, *¿Tiene un poco de agua para mí?*"

Maud handed Buck her canteen. "Have some of mine. Easy. This is all we have."

"His name isn't Paulo." A rider behind them spoke in English. "It's Palo."

The rider, a young, straight-backed man, rode past Palo and joined Buck.

"Palo? Stick?"

"That's right."

"Who are you?"

"Juan Ramón Ruiz, at your service."

"If you're at my service, you can close your goddamned eyes while I ride away."

"Please, Sir, not in the presence of a lady."

"She can come with me if you want, At my service."

"Don't swear in the presence of the lady."

Buck looked at Maud. She nodded primly.

"It's true, I ain't much for cursing. My own mother would have flattened the back-side of your head by now. Then she'd get the strap to the backside of your backside. Things being what they are, I don't have much to say about it."

"The men call her *La Reina*, Mister Buck. You should treat her accordingly."

Buck bent over laughing, his hands to his face. "You're telling me...I got to hear this now. You're telling me that you kidnap this woman, steal her child, take her food, kill her husband..."

Ruiz looked at Maud.

"...and you gonna call her a goddamn queen? I think Queenie may take off your goddamned head."

"The men call her *La Reina* because of her noble behavior."

Maud wrinkled her forehead. "Noble. That's a first."

"It's because you never complain. Yes, it's true that all this has happened. Yes, if you must, you have been treated indifferently."

"You are indifferently full of a cartload of steaming horse shit." Buck was showing his teeth.

"But she never complained. The men complain all the time—in private. They are sick, hungry, exhausted. But they see Miss Maud, how she stays silent in the face of these troubles, how she rides her horse—now her mule—and they respect her. Villa tells them they should be like her. He thinks very highly of her."

"Well, I think you should get off your horse and kiss her ass, if you feel that way." Maud turned away from them. "Not interested."

"Trust me, Mister Buck. Just because I speak to you in English and with deference, I will not hesitate to slice your head from your shoulders before you finish another foul-mouthed sentence."

"Kill a man for cursing. You're delicate."

They rode in silence for a while, the sun beginning to arc past noon.

"It's true," Maud offered. "I learned hard never to complain. My daddy wouldn't have it. I never heard my mother say a word about something that wasn't her own work, except for learning me and my brothers.

About misfortunes, she wouldn't say a word. She use to tell me, Never complain because complainin' ain't no kind of pretty picture."

"If I didn't complain, folks would think I was a deaf mute."

"Well, truth be told, there were times my mother was fiercely silent."

"My mother was fairly like that herself, but my granny, good God, she knew something about uttering her dissatisfaction."

"My daddy, he would swear and cuss like the devil. And he could find fault better than any judge and punish to boot. But not my mother, and she wouldn't have it from me. Or the boys."

Buck shook his head and laughed. "My granny, when she got angry, my mother would get quiet and stone-like, and Granny would get going. Like, say, you burned some food on the stovetop. She'd look at it, push it around a little. Then she'd look at you and sort of rear back her head and get after you. No curse words, not much. Mainly curses."

"Like spell curses?"

"Like fear of the Lord because after I'm tired from kicking your ass down every street in town, he's gonna take over for me. You got the feeling like God would cooperate just out of trepidation."

"Nothing like that from my daddy. Just cuss this and cuss that."

"Well, you see, that doesn't really get the job done, does it. That way, there's some shame, but there ain't enough fear. Granny'd go for outright terror."

They rode.

"For example, one day, this fellow comes to our doorway, looking for my sister, a little older than me. I'm with my mother in the front room, and I come to door when he knocks. I go to the door and open it. He's a nice enough fellow, nice face, pretty smart clothes. He asks me all proper if my sister is at home. My mother, she starts to get up from her chair to talk to him, but then Granny comes in the room from the kitchen and she's wiping her hands on her apron, rubbing them really hard. My mother gets that stone look on her face and sits down again. And Granny starts, 'You goin' to spend a little time with my granddaughter? You think that's goin' to happen? Well, let me tell you something.' And this poor fellow is stepping backwards, staring around like somebody's going to help him. Uh uh, not us."

Maud could see a rider heading their way at a pretty fast clip, racing across the mesa toward the mountainside. Maud lifted a finger to point him out to Buck. Buck nodded.

"Anyway, so she says, you go out with her and lay a finger on my grandchild, and so help me, I will hunt you down, and I will find out which finger touched her first, and I will cut that finger from your erring hand, and I will smoke it like a cigar while I watch the very devils of hell make shorter work with what little manhood you might have sprouted.' She liked going for a fellow's manhood. 'You don't think I can tell a cevil what to do?' she tells him. 'Oh, yes'm,' he says.

"Then she put God to work. 'You believe in God, don't you, young man?' she says. 'Oh, yes'm.' 'Well, let me tell you what kind of special hell the Lord has for those who bother me in particular.' Then, you know, she'd get on to the normal God's gonna get you, whack you around. 'You go to church?' 'Oh, yes'm.' 'Well, I will pray God that he put your name in the preacher's sermon about all that's wrong in the world. All the people in that church will slide down the pews away from you. Forever. Do you understand me, young man?' See? No cussing, just terror."

"How about that boy? How did things work out with your sister?"

"She never married. Takes care of mother."

A cold wind slid off the mountainside. Maud's mouth was dry, her tongue swollen and her eyes stung. "Your granny ever curse you?"

"A few times."

"Did she ever say anything about an army coming out of hell, robbing you of everything you got in the world and then dragging you off with them?"

"Does feel familiar in a way."

Maud wrapped her reins around the saddle horn, tightened her *serape* around her neck and closed her eyes. She was woken by shouts to the rear. She looked about. The rider she had spotted had intercepted the middle of the column and was riding with Villa.

Ruiz called to Maud. "Ride into that canyon. We're staying here for the rest of the day."

The wind hadn't stopped. It picked up dust off the canyon floor and bit their skin with cold and sand. The men dropped off their horses and tied them near sage and grass. A few started some fires deeper in the cold gorge. Shortly, nearly all the men were laid out on the floor, covering their heads with their blankets. Villa did not rest. He walked from one group to another, talking to a few men. Soon he was standing in a circle of his colonels, waving his arms, shouting, spitting.

Maud sat against a rock, watching Villa. Buck had already laid himself between some blankets and was nearly warm enough to sleep. Ruiz was sitting nearby. Maud pointed in Villa's direction. "What's he agitating about?"

"A spy from up north, we got some new information."

"A spy from Columbus?"

"Yes. There was an arms shipment to the soldiers there. Villa has been waiting for this."

"Your men don't look so great, do they? You think they're ready to invade America?"

"You're laughing, but you don't know what Villa can do. You don't know what he can get out of his men."

Villa had finished his conference and was walking out of the canyon, passing near Maud.

"*Señor* Villa. *Señor* Villa."

Villa saw Maud lifting her hand. "*Señora,* I could not recognize you under your wrap. And your face, you have turned red! This life is good for you. Riding with me has made you healthier." He smiled widely, sweeping his arm toward the men outstretched around them.

The wind blasted up a swirl of dust.

"I am sun baked. I am not healthier"

Villa seemed not to hear her. "No one is bothering you, I think."

"I am a captive. You are bothering me."

"I think in a day or two, you will be ready to fight with us."

Maud was silent, uncomprehending. "I will fight with you now."

"Fight for us, not against us."

"Not likely." She spoke in English, gazing up at him.

"*Señora* Maud, if you are tired now, you will not make it with us the whole way. You will drop dead like some of these weaker ones. They cannot get up on the saddle again, so we leave them where they fall.'

"You think I'll die."

"We will leave you where you fall."

"I will outlast your men. *Señor,* I will outlast you."

Villa stroked his mustache "I doubt it."

"And when I do?"

"I have told the men to leave you alone, not to trouble you. When the battle is over, and we are all rich, I will give you one hundred dollars in gold."

"I don't want any money from you."

"And I promise you this. You will have safe passage in my territories."

"May I have safe passage now?"

"When the battle is over, *Señora* Maud."

Maud lifted her bound hands. "In the meantime?"

Villa pulled his knife and cut the tether between her wrists.

MARCH 6

I'm keeping my breasts filled. For when I see Johnnie.

He'll be glad of that.

I keep leaking, but I don't want to dry out. I want to feed him when I see him again.

He'll need to be comforted, all right.

Had a dream, a bad one.

What was it?

I was in a chair, kinda tied to it, and my hands and my feet were chopped off.

Chopped off?

Yeah, clean as can be. Some blood on my dress. On my lap.

Who did it?

Don't know. Nobody was around. I was just sitting there.

Did it hurt?

More like it stunned me. I was sitting there stunned like I'd been knocked in the head. My mouth hanging slack like an idiot.

That's a bad dream indeed.

Am I going to see you again, or are you gone for good?

I don't know. Gone for good, I guess.

You're gone now, ain't you.

I reckon as much.

They shot you, you know.

Just like that?

Just like that.

Palo shook Maud's shoulder. "*Ya es hora de montar, Señora.*"

It was the middle of the night. The moon was thickening, brightening the canyon walls against the black sky. Maud sat up and pulled her *serape* over her head. Palo had already saddled his horse and was lugging Maud's saddle to her mule.

"*Puedo hacer eso.*"

"We have to move."

Ruiz walked his horse toward them.

Maud stood. "Villa ain't not much for sleep, is he?" She spoke in English so Palo ignored her.

Ruiz smiled. "The *federales* sleep at night. Buck, get up." He nudged Buck's length with the toe of his boot. "Get up." He stepped on to his stirrup and, resting in his saddle, looked down the canyon. Hundreds of men were quietly rolling their blankets, tugging at saddles, mounting their horses.

Nearby, Hernandez raised his voice. He was standing over a supine man, threatening him. The man pulled his blanket around over his face. Hernandez drew his sword and slapped the covering with its broadside. The man cowered, pleading but wouldn't stand up. Hernandez joined them. Hernandez swatted him a few more times. The man whimpered but did not stand. Hernandez caught the blanket with his sword tip and yanked it free from the man. Hernandez, rat-faced and angry, shouted, "Get up before we kill you."

As the young soldier stood, her hair fell out at length past her shoulders, the outline of her breasts and hips now more obvious in the darkness. She stood erect, pulling her shoulders back. "What the hell?" Cervantes raged. He looked at Hernandez. "What is this *puta* doing in our ranks?"

"Fighting for Villa." She lifted her chin.

Hernandez slammed her on the shoulder. "I should kill you. Sneaky bitch. Who told you you could ride with us?"

"Enriqueta!" Palo rushed to her. "Enriqueta, what are you doing? You'll get yourself killed."

"Coming to her rescue, Palo?" Cervantes laughed. He tapped Palo's upper arm away from her.

"Please, sir, she only wants to fight. Let her ride up front with us. With us. She won't be any trouble."

Cervantes assessed Palo's face, then Enriqueta's, and then walked away. "Let's leave them. Hernandez. They'll both be dead shortly."

Enriqueta took the old man's hand. "*Gracias*, Palo."

Ruiz rode up to them. "Get mounted. It's time to go."

Maud motioned to Buck, showing him her freed wrists. He lifted his and let her work at the knot. Ruiz watched without comment.

They rode out of the canyon, and the column, at first bunched together, began to stretch out as they followed the trail along the foothills of the mountains, Maud and Buck taking the lead, Ruiz and Enrequita behind them. They rode silently for hours in the cold blue night, sometimes sleeping in the saddle.

At dawn they came to an adobe house, the center of a small ranch. As they neared it, some riders from behind them raced forward, dismounting when they got to the front door. They entered and exited in a minute, waving to the column. "Nothing here." The house was already destroyed, its timbers burned, its walls blackened and windows smashed. An old man watched from a field, standing near a goat. One of the riders went to him. The old man shook his head and pointed northward.

The rider returned to the column, found Villa and reported. "The old man says there are some Americans over the hill with some cattle."

Villa grimaced. "Find them and kill them."

"The cattle?"

"Kill the cowboys. Keep the cattle."

The rider looked at Villa.

"*¡Adelante!* Take about ten men, just to be sure."

The rider nodded and returned to the others who had advanced on the house. They galloped toward the hills to the north. The rest of the column had reached the house, and Villa ordered the men to dismount and rest.

Maud and Buck sat together on a section of porch that hadn't been burnt. Maud had clamped her mouth tight with weariness and thirst. Not so Buck.

"You ever read the funny papers?"

Maud stared at the ground in front of them.

"You know, the funny papers?"

"I don't know any funny papers."

"In the newspaper. The funnies."

"I'm not following you."

"They're funny drawings, cartoons."

"I guess I've seen them."

"Well, your name is Maud, right?"

Maud waited.

"Your name is Maud and you're riding that mule."

Maud waited.

"Well, that's funny, see, because there's a funny about a mule named Maud."

Maud angled her face a little toward him.

"That's what it's called. It's called And Her Name Was Maud, something like that. I saw it the last time I was up north."

"I must've missed it."

"Well, it is as funny as all get out. I swear."

"What's it about?"

"This mule named Maud."

"Uh huh."

"Well, the mule is kind of a cuss, you see. And its owner is named Si Slocum, and he's always trying to get Maud to cooperate, but Maud's a mule, so it does as it sees fit. And the owner, he gets in a tizzy, and then Maud kicks him."

"Kicks him?"

"Yeah, kicks him like a son of bitch. And he goes flying. That's the funny part. She always kicks him. Or somebody else that's molesting her."

"A lesson for us all, I reckon."

Buck folded his hands. "Well, I leave you alone if that's what you're saying."

Maud looked at the ground. "I guess I should look Maud up next time I'm up in the States."

"That's right. You might like it."

"Pretty optimistic, next time I'm in the States."

"What do you mean?"

"I mean, actually I don't figure I'll outlive this trip."

"Aw hell, woman. You're going to kick this problem in the ass. You have nothing to worry about. Don't give me down in mouth."

"You're a fairly cheery fellow for someone who just landed in this mess."

"My nature, I guess."

Maud went to her mule and untied the dusty chunk of meat that was hanging from the saddle horn. She sat back down near Buck and bit off a little piece of flesh. She chewed and swallowed hard. The meat was turning rank, causing her stomach to lurch. She tossed it aside.

"I haven't eaten decent in five days."

"You got to keep your strength up."

"Not with that carcass. I may be starving to death, but I can't eat that."

"I don't know how these boys here do it."

Maud crossed her arms on her lap and put her head down. She was awakened a little latter by the return of the riders Villa had dispatched. They returned shouting and bragging. "*¡Los encontramos! Matamos a los yanquis!*" They were wearing some different shirts and jackets, some new boots.

Buck was still sitting beside her. "Right now, I'm grateful that my clothes are so ratty. No temptation for these boys."

"I guess none of them wanted my dress. Maybe Enriqueta."

"I kindly doubt it. No offense."

She pulled aside the front of her *serape* and lifted the floral cloth off her knees, inspecting it. It was khaki with dust.

"None taken." She put her head back down.

A few minutes passed. Without looking up she said, "I want my baby."

They mounted and rode through the remainder of the morning, Buck hanging back a little with Ruiz. He spoke to him in English.

"Tell me why the old fellow is called Palo. Stick, right?"

"It's a long story."

"I'll let you know when I've had enough."

Ruiz thought for a minute.

"There was a woman, you ever heard of her? Her name was Teresa. Maybe twenty-five years ago, she was a healer in Sonora. Santa Teresita de Cobora."

"Before my time."

"She was a mystic. She saw visions, the end of the world, the end of Mexico. It was during the Diaz days. She prophesied against the government, said they would be washed away in a flood. Which, I guess, they were, after a fashion. But the main, what should I say, the main aspect of her life was that she healed people."

"She was some kind of nurse?"

"No, a healer. No training. She looked at them, put her hands on them, and prayed. And they would be healed."

Buck cleared his throat.

"They were mainly Indians, Yaquis, others. Very desperate people. Poor."

Ruiz called in low voice, "Palo, come and ride with us."

Palo slowed and let Maud and Enriqueta ride ahead.

"What?"

"*Eres un indio, ¿no?*"

"*Mexitzo. Maya y mexicano.*"

"And you went to Santa Teresita for help."

"This is the Palo story?" Buck asked.

"*¡Vamos! Dile a él porque yo no le voy a decir correctamente.*"

They rode silently for a few minutes.

"When I was a young man, I lived in Tomochic, you know, down south a little. My wife and I could not have children. So she wanted to go to to see Santa Teresita because all her family said she could help. Some people from our village had already traveled to see her, and they got better. I said, let's ask the Father what we should do, but my wife said that the priests did not care. I did not know what to think, but I said, sure let's go.

"So we traveled to Sonora to see her, us and some other people from Tomochic. There were a lot of people around her home. It was just a little house in the village, nothing special. At the front door, there was a line of people. One after another, they would go in and then come out happy. My wife got in line, but I stayed a little distance away. I sat with the Tomochic men. We were very quiet. We are quiet people, you know. Not so much like Mexicans. We sat and watched without saying a word.

"My wife goes inside. Then a little later she comes out and walks up to me. In front of my friends she says, Teresita wants to see you. And she gives me a little smile. I looked at my friends, and they looked at me. Then one old guy points with his lips to say go. So I got in the line."

Palo stopped talking for a short while. He opened his canteen, tilted his head back and let a few drops of water drip into his mouth.

"I was a little afraid, I have to admit. It was dark inside, and there were men around the door for protection. There was a priest there, but he was just watching what was going on. He wasn't doing anything religious. I could tell he was angry the way he walked around looking at people and talking to them. So I was afraid of Teresita and I was afraid the priest was going to curse me. I didn't want to have to talk to anyone."

Buck asked, "Why was the priest so worked up?"

"Because Teresita was doing this by herself with her family. Not with the church. So at first the priests thought, Oh, she's holy and tried to tell her what to do, like go to the church and have prayers and masses. But she said no. She didn't like the church because what it did to the people. She said the church and Diaz were thieves, the same band of thieves. I didn't know what the church had done. I just wanted to have some babies.

"Anyway, when I was in line, the priest comes up to me and says, stay away from her. She's a *bruja*. I said, so what to him. That's not bad. And he says she will put my soul in danger. I was young, so I got nervous. I looked over at my wife who was standing by my friends. She waved me on, like go ahead. I told the priest that my wife would put my neck in danger. He called me ignorant, but he left me alone. A man at the door told me to come into the little house.

"It was very bright outside but dark inside so I could hardly see anything at first. There was Teresa, sitting in the center of the room. There wasn't any other furniture. She had a beautiful voice. 'Come here,' she said, and it was like her voice pulled me to her. I lost my strength. I kneeled in front of her. She was like the Virgin to me."

Palo fell silent. The sun had risen high, nearly midday. There were few sounds but the clatter of hooves on the trail. Occasionally, a head of cattle would low from the rear. The men, hundreds of them rode in stoney silence.

Buck waited. "Well, what happened?"

"She put her hands on my head and prayed for me."

"Did it work?"

"Yes, well, we had babies after that, so I think so. Anyway, that's the story of how I met Santa Teresita."

Again they rode silently.

A horseman was riding up the trail toward the column at a gallop. When he reined in his horse at the top of the column, he looked at Maud and Enriqueta with some confusion. Behind them he found Ruiz. "Where's Villa? Quick!"

"Just ride down the line. You'll find him. Is there a problem?"

The rider spurred his horse and with a flick of his reins was gone.

"Wonder what that's about." Buck watched him pass along the stalled column, calling for the general.

"You know, Palo, I didn't ask how you met that woman. I wondered about how you got your name. Your nickname."

"Palo, what are the men talking about?" Enriqueta wheeled her horse toward him.

"*Ay, dios mio.* How much of this do I have to repeat? Everybody knows this story."

"I don't," said Buck.

"What story?" Enriqueta said.

Maud tilted her head.

"Go on," Ruiz said. "Tell them."

"You're the one who wants to be so proper around women."

"You can tell the story appropriately." Ruiz turned to Maud. "This is really a story about the beginning of our revolution."

"*Ay, dios.*" Palo put his hands to his face. "Enriqueta, you tell them."

"Tell them what?"

"Phew, why I'm called Palo."

"How should I know? I thought it was because you have a big *carajo*."

"*¡Ay!*"

Maud raised her eyebrows. Buck laughed.

"Well, isn't that it?"

"I don't know. No, that's not why."

Ruiz gestured to him to continue.

A voice from the rear commanded them to start riding again.

Palo closed his eyes and swallowed. "A little later, maybe. I am tired, very thirsty now."

They rode quietly till mid afternoon when they found a small canyon to rest in. Exhausted men fell to the ground, their horses still saddled. Few spoke, only Villa and colonels, who huddled around the general. Maud watched Villa rage in the distance. The men lying around her were already snoring.

Do you think it's safe to go back?

Yeah, some Mexicans from Chihuahua were talking at the sawmill. They said things had calmed down because of Carranza.

Do we have enough saved?

I think so. Enough for about fifty head.

It'd be nice to get out of El Paso.

Sure. Johnnie would like it out there on the ranch. Wouldn't you, little fellow?

My folks say they won't go back.

Well, that's all right. They're settled again. I don't want that land to go to waste.

When Maud awoke, it was twilight. There were dozens of fires up the canyon. Men were huddled around them. Others were slicing up sides of beef and passing them out. Buck was pushing a hunk of meat on a stick into a flame. Maud walked over to the man doling out the meat and took a bit. She sat beside Buck.

"Villa told me he expected I'd fight for him by now."

"Against Americans?

"Yup."

"That your inclination?"

"Not hardly."

"What is?"

"To find my Johnnie. Get back to my folks."

"Where are they?"

"I got a brother in New Mexico. Silver City. And my ma and pa are in Arizona, logging."

"That your business?"

"Till recently. Now I guess I'm a revolutionary." Maud paused. "Villa said I could travel anywhere I wanted in his territories after the war."

"You want to go back?"

"Well, I just realized, I was thinking he meant Chihuahua. But I think he meant America. After the war."

"Good Lord. He's got some dreams."

Maud dropped her meat on a branch near its burning end. "Indeed, he does. I reckon that means you, too."

"Me what?"

"He'd free you up to travel anywhere when this is over."

"Truth be told, I'm not all crazy about going up north again," Buck said.

"How come?"

"It wasn't all that wonderful for me up there."

"Did you get in trouble?"

"Naw, just tired of being dogged around."

"Where are your people?"

"Alabama. Sharecropping. Then we moved to town."

"I was born in Alabama. My daddy's a sawyer from there."

"That's funny. I thought you had a familiar way of talking."

"We moved to Oklahoma when I was a kid. Then New Mexico. You say I still talk like I was from the south?"

"Yeah. A little. You don't move your mouth. You sound the same way when you talk Spanish."

"As long as people understand me. And you should talk. Half of your Spanish is just swear words."

"Hell, that's not Spanish. That's Mexican."

The colonels walked up and down the canyon, gathering the men's attention. "Villa wants to speak! Villa wants to speak!" The men drew together into a half-circular audience around Villa, who stood with his back to the canyon wall, a small fire between him and his audience.

He surveyed the exhausted faces around him for several minutes. "Maybe you all have heard what happened today!" He gave a log on the fire a short kick and watched it spark and flame up. His face glowed in its light.

Men looked at him blankly. "No? Well, I will tell you now what I heard. Yesterday in El Paso, the Americans burned my friends alive." He watched the effect of the news on his audience. *"Algunos de mis amigos, algunos generales de la revolución. ¡Amigos suyos!* They put them in jail, right there in El Paso. They locked them into cells. Then they poured gasoline on them, everywhere, and lit a match. Whoosh! The whole jail went up in flames, *una tormenta de fuego!* And our friends, our countrymen screamed for their lives while the gringos let them perish."

Villa nodded to shouts of anger and astonishment. He wiped his mouth and smiled. "Remember the raid on the train? Cervantes took care of the American engineers who were coming to strip us of our land and money. When the Americans heard about this, they arrested Mexicans, our friends, to pay us back. People who never did anything wrong." Villa screamed. He choked. *"¡Eso es de los gringos! ¡Eso es lo que son! ¡Se llevaron a nuestros amigos, y los quemaron vivos!"* Villa leaned forward toward the crowd. "I hear their voices, the sounds of their screams. Do you hear what their blood is calling for? Do you hear them? *¡Justicia! Justicia y venganza!"*

The crowd joined him, mustering energy. "Revenge! *¡Viva Villa!"* Then they fell silent. "A few more days, and we begin our invasion. I call on each of you—*¿Están cansados? ¿Tienen sed? ¡Esto no es nada!* You are about to win honor for yourselves. You are about to win an honor unimaginable for Mexico."

"*¡Viva México!*"

"Two more days of ricing. Then we will turn every gringo we see into a torch. Every gringo into a torch, to revenge the deaths of our friends. Gather your strength, men."

Maud pulled her meat away from the fire and blew on it before taking a bite.

MARCH 7

They began riding after midnight. Their horses followed the trail while Maud and Buck dozed in their saddles. Maud woke to tighten her *serape* around her.

"I keep searching my mind how I'm going to get my baby back." She spoke above a whisper.

"What's that?"

"My baby. He's still down on the ranch, I expect."

Buck rubbed his face. "Who's taking care of him?"

"We had some Mexican help."

"How you going to get back down there with all this going on?"

"I keep wondering. How about you?"

Buck was quiet a bit. "I'll just go on back and start over. I think my wife'll stay there till I get back. With the children."

"That's what we did, a couple of years ago. Red Flaggers drove us off the ranch with their raids. But we figured it was all right to come back."

"I was thinking, to hell with it. I could just take off, go back to the states. I guess I could bring Elena and the little ones up with me. Find some work."

"What about your land?"

"Don't know."

Buck was fully awake now. He turned to see who was riding close behind him.

"Enriqueta. I thought you were going to be killed back there when they found you out."

"Me too."

"You were strong, though. Don't you think so, Maud? She was tough."

Maud turned to look at her. Her mule kept its steady, slow pace.

Palo joined them. "Enriqueta has been fighting for a long time."

"No tears." Buck said.

Ruiz spoke from behind them. "She doesn't cry. She kills people."

Enriqueta kept facing forward. "Not recently."

"Soon though."

"I hope."

Buck raised his voice. "Palo?"

"Yes?"

"Don't you want to finish your story?"

"About Teresita? I did."

"About Palo, you didn't."

Palo thought for a few minutes. "When I saw Teresita in the darkness of her house, I had never seen a more beautiful woman."

Enriqueta laughed.

"Seriously, she had eyes that broke my heart. You know how some women have eyes that drill through you? Like Enriqueta's."

"¡Basta!."

In the darkness Maud squinted and then relaxed her eyes.

"Well, Teresita's eyes didn't drill. They pulled you into her. They were dark and soft. I looked at her as if she were a goddess. She was small, slender. She wore a simple white dress, and her face glowed. When she put her hands on my head, I could not control myself. I was submissive as a dog. All my pride left. I had tears in my eyes. I wanted to be with her forever. She moved her hands down to my cheeks and looked into my eyes. Deep. Then something happened that had not happened since I got married."

"What? Well, what?"

"I got a palo."

Ruiz and Enriqueta burst out laughing.

"Wait. What's so funny?" Buck looked around.

"He got an erection." Enriqueta pointed with her chin.

"Oh. A palo. A stick. So?"

"It was unusual for me. That's all. She told me, stand up. I did, and my pants looked like, I don't know, like a tent maybe. They were big and loose, so they stuck out in the front. But I was so happy, and I loved Teresita so much that I didn't care. I walked out into the daylight with my tent, smiling. The man at the front door turned his face away, but when my wife saw me, she clapped her hands and said it's a miracle. *¡Qué milagro!* She ran straight to me. She gave me a big hug, but, you know, not too tight. I was still happy down there. Then my friends saw me, and they started laughing at me with my tent and my wife by my side."

"Well, I'll be damned. I want to meet Teresita."

"So my friends started calling me Palo after that, all the way home."

"You were hard for that long?"

"No, it went away. I got worried that it wouldn't go away. Then I worried that it wouldn't come back. Then back home, my friends told everybody. I should have been embarrassed, but everyone was happy for me. So when they called me Palo, I didn't care. I was happy."

"Wait, so that's why you didn't have babies?"

"Yes, I guess that's right."

"Then you had babies."

"Yes, two."

"Because you had a tent."

"Every time, I'd think of Teresita, and the miracle would happen. Then everybody in the village wanted to see her for whatever was wrong."

They rode in silence for a while.

"Tell them about what happened next," Ruiz said.

"About the massacre? It was summer when I saw her. It was a bad year. It didn't rain for a long time, so there was a drought. The springs were all we had left for water, and they were slowing down. And the crops were bad, small because we couldn't irrigate them enough. We were very worried. In the fall we asked the government for help. We sent someone to the governor. Those people didn't care about Indians. We even sent somebody to Mexico City to talk to Díaz. But everybody was having a hard time, and talking didn't do any good.

"The village was getting bigger because people were losing their land. *Hacienda* owners were taking farms and controlling the water. We called on the *guardia rual* to complain, but they were loyal to the *hacienda* owners.

"The priest was the same. He told us to be patient. Someone said, we'll go to Santa Teresita. She's not a saint, the priest said. *Ella es una bruja. Ella es una puta.* He said we would lose our souls if we listened to her. It seemed like we were in trouble, no matter what. We cursed the priest. ¡Qué *hijo de puta!* That was in the fall.

"So a lot of us went to see Teresita. We all trusted her. She was Spanish, but she seemed to love Indians. So many of us, twenty, thirty of us traveled to Sonora to ask her what we should do. We were like pilgrims. It took about a week to get us all there. It was cold, too.

"We sat in front of her house, and she came out to see us. The oldest man in our group explained to her about our troubles."

Buck said, "Did you get your tent again?"

Maud said, "Stop it."

"She was beautiful like before, like a vision, and all us were staring at her, waiting for her to tell us what we should do. She closed her eyes and began to pray. She stayed quiet for a long time. Then she fainted. She collapsed. And some of us gathered around her to help her up. She stood again and said, '*Tengo un mensaje para ustedes.*'

"She said there would be a great flood that would sweep the land, all across Mexico. There would be death everywhere. Only a few places would be safe. '¿*Quién nos ayudará?*' we cried. '*Dios les ayudará a todos,*' she said. The federal government was the devil, she said. The priests, useless or worse. They will not help you. Of course, we knew that, but it helps to hear it, you know.

"¡*Unámonos!* Stand together, she said, and together you can defeat anyone. God will help you."

Palo was silent for while. There was no sound on the dark trail but the slow clatter and thud of hooves.

"When we returned to Tomochic, there were *rurales* around, checking on us. They acted like we were criminals, asking us questions, eating our food. We hated them. One day, a couple of days after we returned, a *ruale* began to force himself on a girl. The girl screamed, and we stopped him. He got angry and pulled his pistol. We killed him, right there. Which was easy. It surprised us, really. You have a person molesting you, and then of a sudden, you don't. *¡Qué alivio!* But the other *ruales* found out, and the fighting started. We fought back, shooting at them from our houses. It only lasted a day, and they left. We were overjoyed. We shouted, ¡*Viva Santa Teresa!* ¡*Viva Teresita!*

"By the end of December, the day after Christmas, the *federales* came. There were forty or fifty of them. They rode their horses into town, demanding to talk to different people, village leaders. They knew our names, so I think the priest helped them, just like Teresita said. They arrested a few men, and started to leave the village with them. It was like a miracle, then. We all got our rifles and chased after them. We were shouting, ¡*Viva Teresita!* and shooting them down. They fought back, but we killed every one of them.

"Others came. We fought them off always in the name of Santa Teresita. The government got angry at her. They exiled her, her and her father. So Teresita moved up to Arizona so the *federales* couldn't touch her or her family.

"For a year we had good luck." Palo fell quiet again. He licked his lips and coughed a light, dry cough. "I'm very thirsty." Ruiz passed his canteen to him.

"It's all that is left."

Maud lifted her canteen and finished her water.

"I'll end this story in a moment. I'm too tired to keep talking." Palo spoke with his eyes closed. "We fought with the *federales* on and off through the next year. In October the government sent a large division to take care of us. They destroyed the village and killed nearly everyone. Nobody could save us. Not us, not Teresita. I was outside of the village for a few days. When I got back, I saw the desolation. Nearly everyone I knew was killed all in a day. *Devastación completa.*"

Again he was silent.

Maud asked, "What about your wife and two babies?"

"Dead," Enriqueta said.

Maud nodded.

At dawn a rider from behind them instructed Ruiz to stop for a rest where the trail opened into a small mesa. The men dismounted and sat or stretched out in small groups. There was little talk and only a few opened their canteens for final drops of water. Most slept immediately.

After a while five men who had been sitting on the outskirts of the column stood and looked about themselves quietly. They took the reins of their horses and walked them toward the trail. A shout went up from the resting men, a question. The five leaped on to their horses and raced to the south turning back on the trail. Villa stood in the midst of the resting men and ordered Cervantes. "Take some men. Get them!" Within seconds Cervantes was leading a dozen men at a gallop. The resting men watched silently then fell back to sleep.

Later Cervantes and his men returned with five riderless horses. He walked through the crowd, glowering, brandishing two rifles he had taken off the empty saddles. He saw Maud and walked to her, stepping over and around the sleeping men. Maud was leaning against her saddle on the ground. She watched him, her eyes empty with exhaustion. "Are you still alive, *Señora?*"

"Pretty much."

"I thought you'd be dead by now."

"After you."

Cervantes laughed. "Thank you. I have something for you. *¿Sabe disparar un rifle?*"

"That's a Winchester, a thirty-thirty."

Cervantes smiled. "Soon we will be fighting the *gringos*. I will give you this rifle, so you can help us."

"I'll throw it in that *arroyo*."

"If you did that, I'd have to throw you in after it."

"I'll tell you what. You give me a rifle, you'll be the first person I shoot."

"Are you sure?"

"Give it to me. Let's see."

"*Pasámelo. Vamos a ver.*"

"I believe you would." Cervantes walked away, joining Hernandez at a fire.

Buck sat up. "What was that?"

"Just me and my big mouth. I could have had a rifle. By the way, you missed the show."

"What happened?"

"Some deserters."

"Where are they?"

"Out in dirt somewhere. There are their horses."

"That plan didn't work, huh?"

"Not for them. Me neither."

"Looks like it's time to saddle up."

A group of twenty riders mounted and galloped north, leaving the column. The remainder slowly bunched toward the trail until Ruiz led Maud, Buck, Enriqueta and Palo to the front. They resumed their slow pace, Ruiz trailing behind the others.

"Feeling like I have a target on my chest. How about you?" Buck looked at Maud. "That's why we're here, right?" He turned toward Enriqueta.

"How do you like being a target?"

"It's nothing new for me."

"What do you mean?"

"Just that. *Así, que no importa.* I would die a hundred times."

"Once is enough."

"*Por Villa, por yo moruría.*"

"Which?" Buck asked.

"They're the same."

"I don't get the attraction, truthfully."

"You're a *gringo.*"

"Me? I can goddamn assure you I ain't no *gringo*."

"Same. You come down here, steal our land. Of course you don't like Villa. For us, he's salvation."

"I didn't steal shit. I bought my land fair and square. You all are the ones doing the stealing."

"Who did you buy it from? The banks? The *haciendas*? Who lived in your house before you?" Enriqueta's face was twisted.

"It cost me every cent I had."

After a while he turned again. "You'd kill me, wouldn't you.? You'd like to shoot me right now."

"Waiting for my orders."

"Well, goddamn you to hell. Goddamn you, and goddamn every fucking one of you thieves, is all I've got to say."

After some silence, he laughed. "I just wish my grandma was here. She'd have some words for you. She'd fix your problem once and for all. She'd have you riding back south with the devil kicking you every time you turned around. Devil's foot right up your pretty little ass. And your horse's ass, to boot."

"Pretty?"

"Don't you start that shit. Fuck you, fuck you all. I'm too tired for this shit anyway."

"Your grandmother might understand me more than you do."

"Don't you bring up my grandma, or I'll be the one killing somebody."

About noon Maud saw a rider approaching. As he neared she saw he was an American. He passed them, nodding to the women, and spoke to Ruiz.

"What's going on here? Who're ya'all?" He asked in English. Then in Spanish, "*¿Quién es el jefe aquí?*" He smiled and then looked up wide eyed as riders rushed upon him without a word. In a moment he was off his horse, lying on his back.

He stood up and dusted himself off, looking from man to man, each holding a pistol at him. "What the hell?" He turned to bolt off the trail, but Cervantes shot him through the shoulder. The American fell, gushing blood, but stood again. He ran, stumbling forward, his arms flailing. Cervantes allowed him to get a little distance then shot him again. He fell then stood again. Cervantes galloped up to him, grabbing him by the hair. His horse reared, but Cervantes kept his grip, yanking the man up, tearing out a handful of hair. He fell again, got up and stumbled forward. Cervantes shot him in back. He fell. A few others rode up to his body and shot it.

They rode back to the column. As Cervantes passed Buck and Maud, he said, "*Práctica*. For Columbus." Maud stared straight ahead, loosely slapping her reins against her mule's neck. The mule began to walk, and Buck's horse followed. Maud could not speak. Buck was holding his hands to his face, his shoulders heaving.

Later in the afternoon, they rode into a large canyon.

Maud recognized it. "This is Boca Grande."

Palo nodded.

"Columbus is just a bit up north."

Palo nodded again and looked at her.

Inside the canyon the riders who had raced ahead earlier met them with over a hundred horses. Maud noticed their new clothes, stripped from cowboys who had tended the herd. Villa rode to meet them and admired the rustled horses. He stepped off his mule and walked up to a paint stallion, glossy black with sprays of white across its forehead, withers and thighs. He patted its neck, pursing his lips and talking to it. Then turned to the rustlers, giving them an order, pointing to the paint.

MARCH 8

"*Despierte, señora. Ya es hora de montar.*" Palo stood over Maud, lit by firelight. "Time to go." She didn't move. "*Señora.*" No response.

"Maud!" Buck yelled. She sat bolt upright.

"Jesus, Maud, you scared me. I thought you was dead."

"Close enough," she muttered. The night was bitter cold and black. She slumped her shoulders and started to rub her face to wake herself but groaned in pain. In the dark she stared at her hands. They were swollen, her fingers thick. Her face ached from sun. She faltered when she stood. "I may have had enough of this."

A few words were enough to make her close her mouth. Her lips were baked, raw, her tongue sticky. She worked her mouth to find some moisture. Palo watched her. "*No tenenmos ninguna gota de agua. Ninguna.*"

When all the men were mounted, they left the mouth of the canyon and picked up the trail again. They rode through the night in silence, hundreds of men with hardly a word. Now and then a rider would slide off his horse. The riders nearby would stop until he mounted again and then would ride again, wordlessly plodding northwest.

A hint of light glowed behind the mountains to the east. In the darkness a rider began to sing. Maud recognized his tremulous voice.

Oh, I ride with the valiant *Dorados*
I give my life, I give my breath

I ride with the Northern Division
To free Mexico or death

From rape Villa freed his sister
from the rich man's grasp.
Like him we Villistas must ride
To free Mexico at last!

Arriba, Villistas! Arriba la Revolucion!
For Villa and country we cry
Vive Villa y Viva su gente!
To free Mexico we will gladly die!

Another rider said, "Yes, that's much better."

"Thanks, I think so too." There were some mummers, and again the column grew silent.

Johnnie. Ed, watch Johnnie walk. Come here, Johnnie. Come on, sweetheart.

Ruiz and Enriqueta were talking, riding a little behind Maud and Buck. Palo lagged behind, his horse trailing for lack of encouragement.

"You've known Palo a long time."

"Since I was a little girl."

"Same village?"

"Nearby. He became a legend."

Maud turned her head to hear.

"After his people were killed, he became a bandit. He was one of the first to join Villa's gang."

"When Villa was a..."

"They rustled horses and cattle."

"Uh."

"Then they joined Carranza. I heard all this from my father. If you asked anyone in my village about Palo, they would think he is still a young man, a phantom."

Ruiz turned to find Palo, nodding on his horse. "Now he's guarding a woman. Or supposed to be."

"*Para la revolución. Esto está bien ...*"

A few minutes later, "You're a woman."

Enriqueta waited for him to finish his thought. "Is this something you need to worry about?"

"No. No. It's not that. But how did you..."

"It's simple. I would be ashamed not to ride with the Northern Division."

"What does Palo say about this?"

"He wants me to wear a dress."

"Just that?"

"He thinks what Villa thinks. I shouldn't fight. Mainly, though, it's the *pantalones* that bother him."

After a few minutes, "*Él quiere protegerme.*"

"*Por supuesto.* Are you afraid?"

"Of tomorrow?"

"Yes."

"No."

"Do you think we will win?"

"*Claro que sí.* What else can I think?"

They rode northwesterly across a flat of creosote bushes, spindly black against the khaki earth. Away from the mountains now, it was easier to see their numbers, the hundreds of raiders, no longer riding single and double file. They began to group into small divisions. Villa and a few colonels galloped from one bunch to another, Villa forcing his mule ahead of the horses. Maud watched his progress as he neared them. He looked small on his mule, crowned with his little straw hat.

Buck nudged Maud and pointed to a cowboy who rode toward them from the north. "Another visitor."

The cowboy ran his horse toward to the group Villa was addressing and then stopped at a distance. "Hey, hey. Pancho!" he shouted. "*¿Me recuerdas?*" He smiled and waved. With a word from Villa, Cervantes, Hernandez and three others intercepted him. Cervantes raised his pistol and shot him through the neck. The cowboy fell backwards off his horse. He got to his feet and began to run away, but Cervantes galloped to him and shot him in the back. The cowboy dropped face down, his arms thrown forward. Cervantes called the other riders to him. Then he spurred his horse toward the body. The horse stopped, the cowboy at his front hooves. Cervantes squeezed his knees into the sides of the horse, but it reared away from the body. Again, he prodded the horse to the body. The horse, skittish, stepped on its back and then skipped over it. Cervantes reined it around and made it step on the body again.

The other riders joined him, one by one, managing to make their horses step on the body. Villa called out to all the raiders nearby to join him. "Come here. Come here!" He rode up to the cowboy's body and made his mule step on its back. "Here's a *gringo* who thought I was his friend! Here's my gringo friend." He pointed to the corpse, now broken, its chest smashed. "Come on! Greet our *gringo* friend!" One by one, dozens of raiders rode over the body as if engaged in a ritual celebration, whooping and turning to witness the damage their horses' hooves had created.

Maud and Buck watched without a word. The head, eyeless, was crushed open, the mouth smashed agape, the chest's back sliced open, exposing spine and ribs. Buck doubled over the side of his horse to wretch. Maud's eyes dulled as she looked away. A final rider shot the body as his horse pass over it.

"*¿Alguno de ustedes tiene amigos gringos?*" Villa laughed. "Now you know what to do with them!" The nearby riders laughed. They rode forward, leaving the body. Maud kneed her horse forward, and Buck followed.

"That fellow." Maud kept facing forward. "That fellow. They turned him into a pudding."

Buck didn't speak.

"He was nothing but a puddle."

Buck allowed, "That could happen to us, too. You think?"

"I keep expecting so. Not yet, is all I can say."

At noon orders came from behind to break in an *arroyo* they had neared. The raiders seemed to drop from their horses and sink into the soft sand of the dry creek bed. In the center of the *arroyo* ran the damp trace of running water, and men scooped damp sand aside to create small, muddy pools to drink from. Maud sat with her back against the cold sandstone wall of the small canyon, watching the men dig with their hands. Palo sat near her and spoke softly.

"*¿Qué pasará mañana?*"

"*¿Quién sabe?*"

"Can you foretell what will happen?"

"No."

"Do you have a sense?"

"I have a sense that I want to get back to my baby." Maud worked her tongue against the roof of her mouth, pressing it for moisture. "I don't really care to talk right now." She closed her eyes.

"I don't know what to expect," he said. "I want to ask you something."

Maud nodded, her eyes still closed.

"If we live through the fight, where will you go?"

"Back to get my baby. You might be deaf."

"After. Where will you go?"

"New Mexico. Arizona. I've got family."

"You might need help."

"Huh?"

"You might need a man."

"You all shot mine."

"I mean, like a hand."

Maud was silent for a while.

"I don't think I'd have any need for help. I've got nothing to help with."

"I could come with you if you wanted."

"What are you saying?"

"After this, I'm done. I'm no good for fighting anymore." Palo went quiet for a while. Then, "I'm going to stay up north. I'll stay with you."

Maud opened her eyes and leveled a look at him.

"Palo, I'm grateful that you have done what you could for me. But

I have to say, you might think I'm more disposed in your favor than is the case."

"Sorry?"

"You and your *compañeros*. You tore up my life. So I don't want to be your friend. If I'm alive after tomorrow, I won't want to see you again. I think you can understand that."

"You don't know. We have to do this. We are in terror."

"You, you are the terror. Well, not you, exactly."

"No, it's Villa. We fear him. Him and his guards. A lot of these men, they'd flee if they could."

"And you would?"

"I will. Tomorrow."

"Good luck. But not with me." She closed her eyes again.

"Aren't you afraid, Maud?"

"Mainly, I'm tired."

Enriqueta walked to them and slumped to the ground. "There's water there. Dirty."

"No thanks." Palo dropped his head down to his knees. He spoke without looking up. "Enriqueta, are you going to ride in the raid?"

"If I can."

"Maybe you could stay behind and help with the horses."

"Why would I do that?"

Palo fell silent and then fell asleep, his head on his knees. Then he rolled over and slept in the sand.

Riders from the north arrived at a gallop, racing up the *arroyo* until they reached Villa and a gathering of colonels. Maud could hear their report.

"The arms have arrived. They're locked up in the garrison. The soldiers are not organized. They expect nothing."

"How about the Mexicans? Are they still in town?"

"Nothing but *gringos*. Sleepy soldiers and a shipment of guns."

"How many soldiers?"

"Maybe thirty. Not many."

"Where are the guns again?"

"When you come to the town, the garrison is to the east, south of the railroad tracks. Look for the barracks. They are locked up in there."

"Sam Ravel. Is he in town?"

"Didn't see him. His family is in the Commercial."

"A little more rest. We'll mount before sundown."

My folks say they won't go back. They've had enough.

Johnnie. Hey there, Johnnie. Come on, walk to Mommy. Come on.

Do you want to go back? You think the fighting's done?

I dreamed. Ed.

Ed. Can you tell where Johnnie is? Is he safe now? First one who can, goes back to get him is what we said. Can you see him?

I had a dream. Nothing happened. Nothing but a picture. I wasn't even in it. I saw a river, wide and still, and there was quiet music, like a hum, peaceful. I thought of you, I thought of getting back to Johnnie. Tomorrow is going to be bad. I could get killed. I got worried sick, but then I have this dream, and everything is as peaceful as can be. We're all bone weary, Ed. Even Buck ain't talking. What's going to happen to me tomorrow, Ed? Who's going to raise Johnnie?

I wish I had something. Even a hatpin. I'd blind Cervantes. He's got a face like a bulldog. And Hernandez looks like a rat. I wish I had something. I need to warn those people in Columbus.

Maud woke to shouts. Buck lay nearby, slack-jawed. Maud sat up, stiff, and held her head by the temples. She looked up to witness the milling of hundreds of men gathering their blankets and bags. She nudged Buck, then nudged him again. "Wake up. We're riding."

Buck sat up. "Don't want to see this."

"My head is about to split in half."

"Yeah, need some water."

"There's the general."

Villa rode through the crowd mounted on his new paint. He was dressed as he was for the film, wearing a great yellow sombrero with pointed crown. He was dressed in khaki. He wore shiny black boots with silver trim and a silver toecaps. Over his shoulders he had slung two bandoliers stuffed with cartridges, and around his waist was another belt loaded with bullets and two holstered pistols. Off his saddle he had his rifle in a long holster. He shouted, "*¡Oye! ¡Oye!*" and men stopped their preparations.

"Tonight we will cross the border and we will wait till dawn outside of Columbus. At sun up we attack, two divisions, from the south and from the west. We will raze the town. Leave nothing standing. Every man, woman and child you see is your enemy. Make torches of them."

The men stood mute, listening to Villa in the blue shadow of the canyon.

"We are at war with America. Tomorrow we will begin our invasion. It must be a decisive attack. Spare nothing in destroying the town."

Men cheered, and Villa rode toward the mouth of the canyon.

"*Señor* Villa. *Señor* Villa." Maud stood and waved to him. He rode toward her and stayed on horseback.

"*Señora* Maud. I tell you, riding with our company has been very good for you."

"*Señor* Villa. Please, I ask you. Let me go."

"After tomorrow."

"But why not now. I don't want to be killed."

"Neither do I."

"I don't want to be shot at by my countrymen."

"Stay with the horses. That's your job. With that man there." He lifted a finger to Buck. "Keep the horses still. You'll be away from the fighting. It won't take that long. After we take the town, you can do what you want." He smiled at her, open mouthed, his eyes brightening. "Tell everyone you're the friend of Pancho Villa. You will be treated like a queen."

"Like now?"

He turned his paint toward the canyon opening. "*Mañana será un día glorioso para nosotros, para México, para usted también.*" He rode away.

"I wish I had something." She looked at Buck.

"What?"

"I wish I had something to stop that man."

"Villa? You think you're going to stop Villa? You might stop a loco-motive first."

"I wish I could kill him."

"Well, listen to you. You and Enriqueta. Starting to sound the same."

"You think these fools would be riding north if Villa wasn't working them into a frenzy."

"I don't see much frenzy right now."

"You know what I'm saying. If Villa weren't here, none of this would be going on."

Buck sat silently for a few minutes and then rolled up his blanket. "I hope to God you don't have a plan."

"I don't have anything, I wish I had something." Maud tugged the cinches under the belly of her mule and mounted her saddle.

Buck said, "Tomorrow won't be a glorious day if you get us killed."

Ruiz and Enriqueta joined Maud and Buck and they began to ride. Palo followed from a distance. Villa waited at the canyon's mouth and nodded as they passed him. He called to Palo, "Palo. Join your friends." Palo worked at a smile and spurred his horse.

Enriqueta spoke to Ruiz in a low voice. "Why shouldn't I be one of the raiders? I'm as good a fighter as anyone here. Most of these boys, they'd retreat if I gave them an evil look."

"I would."

"I can shoot. I can ride."

"I know."

"Why then? I don't want to hide behind the horses like these grin-gos."

Maud waited a moment. "Do I need to tell you how stupid that was?"

"What?"

"What you just said. Hiding behind horses. This isn't our fight. We didn't volunteer for this." She looked at her eyes and said it in English. "This ain't our fight."

"It should be. If you live in Mexico."

"I'll tell you, Enriqueta. If you need someone to fight, I'm not the one to pick."

"Why not. You're a *gringa*, and you're right here."

"And you have the guns. You have the horse. Give me a gun and a horse. Let's see how that fight turns out."

Ruiz said, "It's true, you know, Enriqueta. That's what Cervantes said. They took Señora Maud because they heard about her."

"Heard what?"

"They heard that you were good with horses and guns. From the people near your ranch."

"And now here I am empty handed and riding on a mule."

"Cervantes thought you'd come around. And Villa."

"Them taking my baby and shooting my husband, that soured me a little. Now I've got this little slip of a girl calling me a coward. I've had enough." She turned to Enriqueta and spoke in English. "You can Viva la revolucion as much as you want. It's not my fight. But if you jaw about me again, I'll start my own."

Ruiz patted the air. "Don't worry yourself. Enriqueta is just talking. Right?"

"I'm going to fight tomorrow."

After a few minutes, Buck ventured, "Enriqueta, you don't have to be so nasty? You're nearly as bad as Hernandez."

"Hernandez is nothing."

"Jesus. Never mind."

"Ask Hernandez why he's the way he is."

"I don't think nothing made Cervantes mean. He probably came out of his mama swinging his damned sword around. Cut his way out, for all we know. Anyway, nobody round here wants to talk to Hernandez."

"Then don't talk to me."

They rode in silence for a while, heading north nearly side by side without a trail across the creosote-dotted plain. The sky, cloudless and still, slowly purpled, leaving an azure rim in the west.

Enriqueta started again. "You live here, you have your babies and your cattle. You know nothing about what is happening."

"That's right. I don't know anything."

"You think...if you had seen what I've seen, you would be fighting too."

Buck wiped his mouth. "Enriqueta, maybe I don't know anything about what's bothering you all. But don't tell me what I haven't seen. I might have seen a few sights myself. I had my reasons for leaving the States." He thought for a moment. "But right now, my head is fit to bust, and I can't work my mouth. Anyway, me and Maud, neither one of us signed up to die for Villa."

Maud nodded. "I don't get the attraction."

"I would do anything for the general. Anything."

"So you've said."

"He raided the *hacienda* my family worked on."

Buck leaned to Enriqueta. "Now see, didn't that make you hate him?"

"No. I stole a horse and followed him."

"Damnation. You're a goddamned fool, Enriqueta."

"I told you. You don't know what goes on at a *hacienda*, the work, what the boss does to you, to your family. My father died sharecropping. If you don't have land, you're somebody's slave. When Villa raided us, it was a relief. I knew if I didn't leave, I'd be a slave."

Maud nodded. "Well, that part seems familiar."

"What do you mean?"

"Ed and me. We came to Mexico to get some land, to be free."

"Yes, yes."

"We saved up a long time to get what we got."

Buck nodded.

Enriqueta spit some air. "*¡Pinche gringos! ¡Pinche gringos* coming to Mexico to get free! *¡Hijo de puta!* Where do Mexicans go to be free?"

Ruiz laughed. "You know, she's right about this. Señor Buck, your house, the one we came to, who built that house?"

"It was there when I came. I bought it."

"From?"

"The bank."

"Where do you think they got it from? You think the guy that built that house is counting your money somewhere?"

Buck was quiet for a moment. "Well, it isn't that great of a house."

Maud's eyes burned with fatigue. She closed them and sealed her lips, working her tongue against the roof of her mouth for moisture. The riders near her grew tight lipped. Only Buck muttered, cursing under his breath.

A terrible aching in the arms, Ed.
From?
Where Johnnie ain't. I feel where he ain't, and my arms ache. My chest. I feel I could die of missing him. And you. It's a terrible, terrible hurt. And my breasts are killing me. I'm a mess, ain't I.
Chin up, Maud.
I barely can hold myself up on my saddle. My head is pounding so.
You get back to Johnnie.
Lord, how I'll squeeze that little boy. This is pushing me pretty hard, this riding. Not even pa pushed me like this.
Another day, it'll be over.
Another day, I might be sitting with you.
You get back to Johnnie.
Ed?

The quarter moon was up, and the cold sky was brittle with stars. Maud bunched her *serape* around her waist and neck. The riders up and down the line were passing orders urgently, quietly. In the darkness they could make out the silhouette of a barbwire fence. A few riders approached it, dismounted, and worked at the wire with pliers. After they had made a few cuts, they motioned the raiders through the opening. A smear of light from the Milky Way glowed overhead, and a few lights shown from outlying ranch houses. The riders, narrowed again into a column, began to veer northwest, Ruiz directing Maud and Buck away from the lights of Columbus.

"We're looking for an *arroyo* on the west side of town. We'll stay there."

About midnight they had gathered, wordlessly, along the steep walls of a draw. The lights of town had been extinguished, and in the darkness officers repeated orders in whispers. "*Manténgase montado. Manténgase despierto. Quédese quieto. Tranquilo.*"

MARCH 9

urrounded by the horsemen in the *arroyo*, Maud watched the raiders maintain their vigil for hours. Finally, a faint trace of light lined the east, and a rooster crowed. In the near darkness she heard hushed orders passed from group to group. She smelled kerosene and saw dark figures pouring it into small tins. She watched as a group of dismounted figures tugged the canvas wrapping off the barrel of a large machine gun. One figure, mounted, cradled its collapsed tripod. Another, mounted, reached down to his partners to take up the barrel. After another spell of quiet, she heard the rush of riders pushing into the crowd. She could see Villa, who spoke in a full voice. He directed half of the divisions out of the *arroyo*, pointing east with both hands and then separating his hands to make a splitting motion. "Wait for the sound of our gunfire before you begin!"

The divisions followed their orders, riding up a low spot in the draw, now careless of noise. When they had cleared out, Villa gave orders to the remaining half. "Once you are past the train tracks, split in two and ride down the streets. *¡Dispárenles a todos!* Make sure the Commercial burns." He turned to the men holding the parts of the machine gun. "Set up in the middle of the main street. Face east. Look for uniforms."

They rode out of the *arroyo*, Ruiz prompting Maud and Buck to follow. Ahead of her, Maud could see Enriqueta push her hair up into her hat and square her shoulders. Palo took up the rear. Out of the *arroyo*, they passed to the west of a low hill, separating them from the town. Villa called to Ruiz, instructing him with a circular wave of his arm. Ruiz returned to Maud and Buck. "This is where we will stay with the fresh horses. This is the remuda. Round up the riderless horses, get them out of the way." He cut his horse away from them and made a quick sweep of a couple dozen horses that the raiders had left. "Pull everything off them except their saddles. Take off their bags." Palo rode by them, lifting bags off their backs and dropping them into a pile. He looked around the circled horses. "Where's Enriqueta?"

They could hear a shout and gunfire. Ruiz smiled. *"¡Aquí vamos!* Get off your mule, *Señora*, and hold the horses steady. Keep them behind the hill."

Maud was mute with fear. Dismounting, she heard an explosion, and the gunfire nearly constant. A train surged toward the town approaching the hillside. Passengers pressed against the windows, a line of shocked expressions, to witness the beginning of the attack. The brakes squealed as the engineer tried to reversed the direction of the train. Failing to stop the engine in time, he released the break and let the train rush past the insurgents and through the town. In the distance Maud could hear the shouts of the raiders. *"¡Viva Villa! ¡Viva México! ¡Muerte a los gringos!"*

"This is madness." She muttered to the forehead of her mule, patting its forelock. She walked her mule around the far side of the hill. The town was alight with fire from its center. By the light of the flames, she could see Villistas riding through the streets, three or four at a time, leveling their rifles at windows, shooting and yelling.

She could make out the figure of a small boy, dressed only in his long johns, running out the doorway of a burning building. He sprinted along the building and into a field, dropping headlong in the distance. A man stood at his door, taking aim as the riders passed. Wave after wave of raiders swept down the street and then turned away down a parallel street to return to the west side of town. Maud watched as a rider dismounted to pour kerosene along the face of the wooden face of a building. He leapt away from the rush of flames behind him and mounted, racing to the end of the street.

A loud snap shocked her mule. It staggered away from her. A bullet had flattened against her saddle close to her head. She pulled its reins and tugged it back toward the remuda.

She found Buck standing with the horses. "We gotta get out of here, Maud."

Ruiz rode up to them. "Get ready."

"What?"

"Here they come!"

"What are you saying?"

A group of riders sped up to them, sliding off their horses as they approached. Without a word, they mounted fresh horses and rode away. "Move those tired ones away from the others. Maud. Maud. ¡*Mueva los caballos cansados!*"

Maud grabbed their reigns and pulled them aside. Another rider galloped up and dismounted. He staggered toward a large rock and leaned against it, wrapping an arm around his stomach. Blood oozed around his forearm, bloodying his shirt, spreading into his lap. He slipped down, seated, facing Maud and Buck, staring at them blankly. His forearm dropped to his lap, exposing a blood-blackened wound.

"¿*Dónde está Enriqueta?* Palo, ¿*Dónde está Enriqueta?*"

Palo walked to the wounded man, drawing his hand over his eyes to close them. "I haven't seen her."

"She's out there, isn't she."

"I guess so."

Among the fresh horses Maud found Frank's mount with his saddle still on its back. She walked to it, stroked the side of its neck and thought. Palo walked to her.

"*Señora. Por favor. Si se va, déjame ir contigo...*" he whispered.

"I already told you about that."

"I can't bear it anymore."

Another group of four raced up to take new horses. "Tell me, tell me."

Ruiz stopped one of them before he could ride away. "How's it going? Tell me."

"Their army. They're useless. They don't have any guns! Just a few."

"How's the town?"

"*¡Fuego por dondequiera!* We've won." He rode away.

In the distance they heard the sound of a different machine gun. It sputtered a few shots and stopped. A few minutes later it began again and stopped. More riders came and left, triumphant, ecstatic with news.

"The army can't get to their guns! They're all locked up! We saw them trying to get into the armory. We're picking them off like crows."

Shortly, the new machine gun was firing steadily. No riders returned for fresh horses. Apart from the sound of the new gun, the gunfire grew more sporadic, then dropped to nothing. A raider returned to the hillside but didn't mount a fresh horse.

"*¿Qué estás haciendo?* Get back out there!" Ruiz shouted at him. The rider merely looked at him and stayed still. Another rider joined him. Then another, bleeding from his shoulder. Soon there were dozens taking refuge from the hillside. Villa came running around the hill. He was waving a pistol. "Get back to the streets. Get back. *¡Dejen de esconderse, pinches cobardes!*" They rode back toward the town but stopped when they were free from his eye line. He walked to Maud with his hand outstretched for the reins of a fresh horse.

"Where's your paint?"

"Dead."

"Shame."

Villa mounted and rode toward the town, yelling and waving his pistol.

The gunfire died to a few bursts. A rider rode slowly up to the remuda.

"What is happening?"

"The *gringo* soldiers are awake."

"And?"

"I'm going back out there to die. So many dead."

The raider mounted a fresh horse and rode away at a saunter. Ruiz yelled after him. "*¡Viva!*"

The air was thick with smoke and the smell of gunfire as the sun glowed against the eastern horizon. The town had become silent except for an occasional pop from a gun and the rush of fire from collapsing buildings. Riders began to stray toward the hillside, some of them bleeding. A couple of raiders staggered up to the remuda begging for horses. *"¡Por supuesto!"* Ruiz said. "Why, what is happening?"

"I think we're done for now."

"¡Imposible!"

One of the riders mounted a fresh horse and kicked its sides, racing it back to the town. The other rider found a rock and sat, his hands to his face.

"Ruiz! Ruiz!"

"Yes, Senora Maud. What is it?" Ruiz watched the seated raider.

"I think I'm done here. Let me go."

"What's this, done here?"

"The raid is finished. I don't want to get killed by the soldiers when they come back here."

"You can't go until Villa says."

"Well, where is he? He might be out there in the streets for all you know."

"Wait till I talk to the general."

A bugle sounded the retreat and then sounded it again. Raiders raced around the hill, shouting, wild-eyed. *Dorados* yelled orders, driving the men south.

Buck edged away from the crush as the retreating raiders gathered behind the hillside. Maud watched as he slid to his side and then lay as if dead. Dust from the horses drifted over him.

Finally, Villa rode around the hill. He yelled at the last group of riders, waving the men behind him forward. *"¡Vayan ya! ¡Fuera!"* He was slumped forward in his saddle. His sombrero was gone, and his cartridge belts were half empty. "Hurry. The army is coming." He turned in his saddle to yell to the riders behind him. *"¡Vayan! ¡Vayan!* Back to Boca Grande!"

Maud ran up to the front of his horse to stop him. "You're done here. It's time to let me go." She shouted over the rush of passing riders, their horses galloping south. Villa turned his horse away from her, but she lurched toward him.

"I'm leaving. Am I free?"

"*¿Por dónde?*"

"*¿Por dónde?*"

"Which way do you want to go? *¿Norte o sur?*"

Maud pointed to the town.

"*Está bien, entonces. Tu estás liberada.*"

"I'm taking my horse, my saddle."

Villa looked again over shoulder to find the last or the raiders gathering behind him. "*Como quieras. Vete.*" He yelled to the last men, "Go, go to Boca Grande. Ride." He looked at Maud and then kicked the sides of his horse.

"You hear that, Ruiz?" Maud turned to find herself alone.

She climbed up on to the back of Frank's horse and rode slowly around the hill. Outside of town lay a house, a corral with tank fed by a windmill. Maud rode toward it. As she neared it, she saw a body on the ground, twisting in pain. It gasped, "*Agua. Por favor. Agua.*" Nearby lay a horse, dead, with a black, silver-studded saddle. Maud dismounted and stood over the man. His nose and cheek had been shot off, and he worked his mouth mechanically, whispering water, water, spitting out the blood that seeped along his lips. Maud recognized the sword that lay in its scabbard, akimbo from the body's hip.

"Hernandez."

"Water."

She knelt, reaching for the sword, gripping its grand hand guard. She slid it free from it scabbard, and stood again over Hernandez, dropping his sword's point to his chest.

"Water."

"Is that your horse? Is that your saddle?"

He moved his lips.

"I'll take that saddle, if you don't mind." She lifted the sword in its direction and then pointed it against his heart.

"Water."

"You're going to die soon enough, Hernandez. I'm not going to help you get there." She let the sword fall flat on his chest and walked to the black saddle. She loosened its cinch, lifted the saddle off the horse's back and lugged it to Frank's horse and dropped loosely on top of the other saddle.

She walked her horse to the tank to let it drink, lashing its reins to a post, and then crossed the property to the house. At the bottom of the porch stairs lay a grey haired man, lying face down, his rifle lying beside him. She knelt beside him and turned him over. He had a bullet hole in his chest, his body slack and heavy. Maud climbed the stairs of the porch and gazed over the property. In the distance she saw another body, waving an arm aloft against the bright sun on the horizon. She rushed to it, finding an old woman wounded in the hip, groaning. She helped the woman to stand erect enough to lean on her. "There, there. Here we go." With small skipping steps, they made their way to the house.

"My husband may be shot. I think I saw him get shot."

"Yes, ma'am. He's over there, I believe."

"Is is all right? What did he say?"

"He ain't all right, I'm afraid."

They made their slow way to the house. The woman fell at her husband, sobbing. "No, no, no."

"Come on, ma'am, let's get you inside." Maud tugged her upward.

"Are you a Mexican?"

"No, ma'am."

"Are they coming back?"

"Who's that?"

"The Mexicans. Are they still here?"

"Naw, they're all gone."

"For good?"

"For now. Let's go. Up you go." Maud pulled her up against her hip and supported her into the house. When they made it to the woman's bed, Maud led her to the edge and let her roll herself flat on the bed, grabbing at her hip, gasping.

"Ma'am, I'm going to get myself some water. I might die of thirst right where I'm standing. Then we're going to get that wound cleaned up.

"What did them Mexicans want with us? What in the blazes were they doing?"

"I'll be right back with some water and rags."

"We didn't do nothin' to them, did we? My husband? Did he hurt some Mexicans that they'd want to kill him?"

"I'll be right back. Now you just calm yourself."

Maud walked to the kitchen and found a pitcher and a bucket of water on a counter. She leaned against the counter's edge and lifted a ladle of water to her mouth. She drank the full ladle's worth, but it wasn't enough. She drank another and stood still a minute, looking out the kitchen window. Then she brought the bucket and a pan to the bedroom.

"Are you one of them?"

"Sorry? Didn't get that?"

"Are you one of the Mexicans?"

"How do you reckon that?"

"From the looks of you."

"No, no. You're in a lot of pain. I ain't a Mexican." Maud began lifting off layers of dress and petticoats to get to the wound.

"Hello. Hello. Mrs. Moore? You here, Mrs. Moore?"

"Help! Help me! I'm in my bedroom!"

A man dashed in, his pistol drawn. He pointed it at Maud. "What's happening here? Who are you?"

Mrs. Moore raised herself. "Sheriff Breen! Thank goodness you're here. I'm wounded and this Mexican is working on me."

"I ain't Mexican. I already told you that."

"Well, what are you?" The man indicated with the pistol barrel that she should move away from the bed.

"I'm American as you."

"Not from the looks of you."

"Stop waving that pistol around. She's been shot here."

"Why'd you shoot Mrs. Moore? You one of the Villa gang?"

"No! Why are you calling me Mexican?"

"Mrs. Moore, you seen your husband?"

"Yes. I seen him. He's dead now, ain't he. Out there in front."

"Yes'm. Sorry to say it."

Mrs. Moore began to heave with short gasping sobs. "Why'd they shoot us up like that?"

"Ma'am, they shot us all up. The whole town's burning, seems like. Some people dead."

Maud began to lift away clothing to clean her wound, but Mrs. Moore clutched at her hip with a yelp.

"Lady, you need to leave her alone. Mrs. Moore. Mrs. Moore. We'll get you to the doctor right away."

Mrs. Moore lay back in her bed and moaned.

"I'm going for help. You stay put, lady. I need to ask you some questions."

He walked to the door. "And I think you'd better let her be. She thinks you're trying to finish her off."

Weariness flooded Maud as she sat on the edge of the bed. She dropped her head to her hands and closed her eyes. Instantly, she was asleep then jerked awake in a panic. She stood, looked at Mrs. Moore moaning on the bed, and saw a movement across the room. She saw her figure mirrored over a dresser and walked toward it.

She could hardly recognize herself in the coppery reflection, her hair dusty, swept back and matted in a bun, her face swollen and nearly maroon with sun. Her *serape* and her dress had turned dust brown like her hair as if she had become almost all one color, the dirt dulling the calico. She put her hands, reddened, her fingers thickened and stiff, to her sore cheeks and gazed at the apparition, looking into her eyes, searching for some familiar feature.

She returned the bed and sat beside her patient. "I ain't what I look like, Mrs. Moore."

"Uh? Uh?"

"I know what I look like to you. But I ain't a raider."

"Who's here? Who's here?"

"We're in here. In the bedroom."

A couple of men, soldiers in woolen uniforms, came to the door. "Is this the wounded lady?"

"This is her. She's shot in the hip here."

"We've got an ambulance. Step aside now."

Maud moved to a corner in the room. "Her husband's dead outside."

"We've already got him. Up we go." One of the soldiers lifted Mrs. Moore in his arms. The other, a sergeant, turned to Maud. "Where'd you learn such good English?"

"Lord."

"Come with us."

The sergeant marshaled Maud out of the house and into the back of a wooden-spoked military truck. She sat on the sidelong bench at the rear opening. Mrs. Moore lay in the center on a stretcher. The sergeant sat facing Maud. The truck lurched forward, and Maud clutched the wooden seat. "I've never been in such a thing."

"Well, welcome to America."

The truck bounced and jerked its way into Columbus.

"I am American."

"You? Me, I'm from the moon."

"I come from Oklahoma."

"All right. Oklahoma. To be fair, I never met a woman from Oklahoma, so you may be telling the truth." The truck bounced, and both of them were jarred off their seats and landed hard. Mrs. Moore groaned.

"Just a few minutes, ma'am."

Maud could see from the back of the truck the smoking remains of the main street. On each side of the packed dirt road, wooden structures burned and smoldered. The air was grey and stung her eyes. She saw a man helping a limping wounded soldier, and she saw pairs of men carrying bodies to the front of a brick building where there lay a row of covered corpses. Another man was dragging a dead raider by the boots, the body's arms leaving straight trails behind him.

The truck heaved slowly over train tracks, past the train station and into the army camp, jerking to a stop in front of a row of tents. "Here we are, Mrs. Moore. These boys'll take good care of you." Maud followed her stretcher into the surgeon's tent. She walked from bed to bed, gazing at the wounded. An officer stood over a moaning man, pressing briskly at the flesh around his leg. Maud stood by his side. "How can I help?"

"Hold his leg out straight, will you? He keeps jerking it around."

The man's pant leg had been cut off, but his boots were still on. Maud tugged at his boot and straightened his leg. The doctor pressed near the wound again while the man moaned. "There it is. That's it." He felt on a nearby tray for forceps.

"I found that woman over there. She's shot in the hip pretty bad."

"All right. We'll get to her in a minute. Just need to sew this fellow up. Now hold him still. That's it. That's it."

The doctor looked up Maud. "What happened to you?"

Maud stared at him.

"You look like hell. Where's this hip wound?" He walked across the tent. "Hello, ma'am. Looks like you got shot. Are you in pain?"

Mrs. Moore moaned. "You're going to be fine." He cut away her dress.

"This funny looking Mexican helped me." Mrs. Moore raised her head off the stretcher.

"Who's that, ma'am?"

"This woman here."

"You're a Mexican?"

"American."

"Where'd you come from?"

"Chihuahua. With the raiders. I was a captive."

"Uh huh." He felt Mrs. Moore's flesh. "Orderly. Can you come over here?"

"Sir?" A young man stood at attention.

"Are you armed?"

"Yes, sir."

"Could you escort this, uh, woman out of the tent and get her to Col. Slocum immediately."

"The colonel isn't on base, sir."

"He's back from Deming. He just got back. Take this raider to him and find some men to assist you. I don't know what to think about her."

"Yes, sir."

"She helped me." Mrs. Moore reached out for Maud's hand. "Thank you."

"That's enough. Let her go."

"She helped me."

"Take her, son. Up to Colonel Slocum's house."

The young man took Maud by the elbow and ushered her outside.

Slocum's house, a little northeast of the burned center of town, was untouched by the raid. The orderly and a couple of soldiers drove her by wagon, Maud seated by the driver, the orderly in the rear. When they arrived, Maud hopped quickly off the wagon before the orderly could rush to help her down. He led her up the porch stairs and announced himself. Slocum came to the door.

"Sir, we don't know who she is, but she says she came with the raiders. She says she was a captive. She was in the surgery tent when we caught her."

"Wait, you didn't catch nothing!"

Slocum looked at Maud's swollen red face and dropped his gaze down along her dirty *serape*. He drew his head back and watched her eyes.

"What do you know about this raid? Are they coming back?"

"I don't know. I don't think so."

"Were you privy to this operation?"

"We didn't have a privy. We were riding all the time."

Slocum looked at her a moment. "You better come inside. Thank you, Private. You can go back to the surgery."

A few soldiers standing in the living room turned to look at Maud. "Mary," the colonel shouted. "Can you join us?"

A woman walked into the living room but stopped short when she saw Maud.

"Mrs. Slocum, can you attend to this woman? What is your name?"

Maud glanced at Mrs. Slocum, then gazed at the floor between them. She closed her eyes and found it difficult to open them.

"Your name? Young lady?"

Maud cleared her throat softly. "Maud. Maud Hawk Wright."

"Would you take Maud and clean her up. Keep an eye on her. I'll need to question her shortly."

Mrs. Slocum crossed the room and, taking Maud by the hand, led her to a bedroom. Standing beside the bed, she reached for Maud's *serape*. Maud stood motionless. "Come on, let's take these things off. Come on." Maud helped push the serape over her head. The serape's opening caught on her hair bun. Mrs. Slocum jostled it free. "Lord, your hair." She turned Maud around and unbuttoned the back of her dress and pulled it off over her head. As Maud stood before her in a cotton slip, Mrs. Slocum looked at the white of her skin on her shoulder and then at the color of face and hands. "Good Lord. What happened to you, young lady?"

"I was a captive."

"You aren't a Mexican, I can see. And those blue eyes."

"I have a son."

"What's that?"

"I have a son. I need to find him."

"You have a son. That's fine. Where is he?"

"In Mexico, back home. Help me."

"In Mexico. Well. Let's take care of that later. I want to get some water on you. Sit down now and I'll fill up the tub with some hot water for you."

Maud sat on the bed and closed her eyes again.

Ed. Ed.

She awoke to Mrs. Slocum's voice. "Come on, dear. Wake up. Goodness. Look at the dirt on that bed. Come on, stand up now. Come to the bathroom and get in the tub. Off comes the slip now. Here we go."

Maud stepped into the tub and sat in the water.

Mrs. Slocum tested the water. "That's about right." She poured a stream of water over Maud's shoulder. It ran down her body, spreading a whirl of brown across the tub. "We've got some work to do." She soaped a wash rag and put it to Maud's face.

"Ah. Ah. That hurts."

"All right. All right. Easy does it. I have some cream to ease that burn." She scrubbed Maud clean and motioned her out of the tub. She patted Maud dry and said, "Lean over the tub." She stood before Maud and began to work her hair loose from its bun. "It's nearly stuck in place." Maud's hair dropped heavily around her head as she leaned forward over the tub. As she leaned, she found Mrs. Slocum's hip and put her weight into her. Her shoulders shook. Mrs. Slocum took Maud's head in her hands and pet her. Maud spoke into Mrs. Slocum's clothes. "You are like a mother. You are like a mother." Her eyes ached.

Johnnie.

"You're leaking milk, you know."

"I know. Believe me."

"You were nursing?"

"Hope to be nursing again as soon as we're done here."

Mrs. Slocum's eyes brimmed with tears.

"His name is Johnnie."

"Pardon?"

"My son. His name is Johnnie."

"All right." Mrs. Slocum wiped her eyes with her free hand. "We'll take care of that soon." She poured water over Maud's head, got more water and poured more water over her head. She felt Maud's weight against her belly.

"Maud, how did you get this dirty? Where have you been?" She poured more water and lathered her hair.

Maud was asleep then awake. Mrs. Slocum twisted water out of her hair and put a towel over her head.

"All right. Let's get some clothes on you."

Maud awoke hours later wearing night clothes, lying covered in a bed. It was still bright daylight, and the house was busy with movement and voices. Shouting had wakened her.

"The men were hungover, sir. Many of them. So they were slow getting up."

"They were drinking hard?"

"Might have been normal, maybe worse. You were gone, so they might have drunk excessively."

"Because I was gone? That is no excuse. Castleman was on duty. There's nothing wrong with me being away from the camp. How the hell would I know this would happen."

"And there's the matter of the keys. The munitions were under lock and key."

"Proper procedure. Who had the keys?"

"I think that's the question, Sir. Maybe Lt. Castleman. But he was in the middle of the fighting."

"Well, the men pried the door open, so they got to the rifles and the machine guns in short enough time."

"The machine gun was another problem, sir. It jammed."

"The Benet-Mercier. Goddamn that piece of shit."

"Lt. Lucas was on it with a corporal. They got it working. They tore through greasers with that. All told, we got about a hundred of them."

"The Mexicans?"

"Yes, sir."

"Castleman's left."

"His column left about an hour ago in pursuit. Also Captain Stedje."

"I sic'd Major Tompkins on them right off. Maybe he can finish them off."

"They're entering Mexico, sir. You're aware."

"I don't give a good goddamn about that."

"Sir, the soldiers reckoned Pancho Villa led the raid."

"They see him?"

"They heard the Mexicans shouting *Vive Villa*."

"Son a of bitch. I hope the pursuit kills that fucker."

"Yes, sir."

"I got someone here. A woman. Rode with the Mexicans but says she was captive. I'm going to work on her as soon as I can. She says they aren't coming back for another raid."

"Not with Tompkins on their backsides, sir."

When Maud woke again, it was dusk, and Mrs. Slocum sat beside her in bed.

"You rested, young lady?"

"Is there water?"

"I'm going to give you tea and some proper food in just a few minutes. Now let's put some cream on your face and hands." She put her forefinger into a jar and dipped out a dollop of white cream and applied it to Maud's reddened cheeks. "There, there."

When she woke again it was night, and the house was dark and still.

MARCH 10

"Maud."

"Maud. Maud. Can you wake up?"

Maud awoke to daylight, bolting upright in terror. Mrs. Slocum was sitting at the foot of her bed.

"The Colonel needs to talk to you. I'm sorry to wake you."

Maud looked about her at the clean, bright room, felt the impossible softness of the bed, inhaled and closed her eyes.

"You slept a long time. My husband has to take up some business with you."

Maud propped herself up, pulled her knees up to her chin, and rubbed her eyes.

"I need to get back to Mexico."

"Uh, Maud. Just wait, now. Don't talk like that."

"I need to get back there right now!"

"Why, Maud?"

"I've got to get back to Johnnie."

"All right, Maud. Let's get you dressed. Then you can tell the Colonel. But, do yourself a favor and be careful how you talk about Mexico."

Maud stood up. Mrs. Slocum eyed her. "I think I have some clothes that will fit you just fine. Stay put."

Maud sat back on the bed until Mrs. Slocum returned with thick woolen clothing draped over her arm. "This ought to do the trick." She stretched a skirt and blouse out on the bed. "What do you think?"

"They're fancy."

Mrs. Slocum clapped her hands together. "Let's get you dressed." She picked up the dress. "Arms up. Off with the nightgown. Here we go."

When she had dressed Maud, she turned her toward a mirror. "Beautiful."

The clothes were stiff and a little large, the sleeves covering much of her sunburnt hands. Maud gazed mutely at her face, dark against the high white collar of the blouse. Her cheeks looked bruised.

"Would you like to eat some breakfast? Come, sit and eat with me." Her voice was singing. She took Maud by the hand and led her to a dining room table. "I'll be right with you, now. Stay put, and Dolores'll bring you some eggs. Dolores, you hear? We need breakfast for this young lady."

"Yes'm."

Shortly, the maid brought fried eggs and bread to the room. She put the plate in front of Maud. She looked at Maud, then at Mrs. Slocum.

"That's all, Dolores. Thank you."

Dolores stood still a moment then turned to the kitchen.

Maud ate quietly, intensely, while Mrs. Slocum watched, sitting across the table. "You've been through quite a trial, haven't you."

Maud wiped her mouth with a napkin. "Thank you, ma'am. I appreciate your hospitality." She stood. "I need to get going."

"What on earth! What's your hurry, Missy?"

"I got to get to my baby. He's down on our ranch."

"Whoa, now. You need to...Colonel Slocum needs to talk to you. He can help you."

"Not really looking for help, thank you. I just need to make sure about Johnnie. I can take care of that myself."

"Colonel. Colonel. Our visitor is ready for the day. Herbert."

Colonel Slocum filled the doorway. "Come, young lady. Let's talk in my office. He motioned to her to follow. He sat in his chair behind a small desk and opened his palm toward another chair for Maud.

"Miss. Or should I call you señora?"

"Mrs."

"Your greaser friends have done terrible damage to our town. I wonder if you're happy about that."

"You talking about the raiders. They ain't friends of mine."

"You came with them. Go on. They're your *compañeros*. Isn't that what you call them?"

Slocum smoothed his mustache.

"They ain't friends of mine. They took me off my ranch, me and my husband and stole my baby."

"Your husband. The two of you joined the spics."

"We didn't join nobody. They shot him. I can show you where."

"They killed your husband. I see." He wrote a note. "And what was his name?"

"Edward Wright. Why are you asking me these questions?"

"Are your men coming back for another raid is what I need to know."

"My men."

"Your *compañeros*."

"I don't think Villa's coming back, if that's what you're talking about. I saw him afterwards. He looked pretty beat."

"You saw him."

"Uh huh."

"You talked to him."

"Yes."

"About."

"About leaving. I asked him could I leave."

"You asked his permission. And what did he say to that?"

"He said stay up here."

"Not to come back with him?"

"That's right."

"Did he give you any orders?"

"Yes, he said stay up here."

"What were you supposed to do up here?"

"Just stay, I suppose. What do you mean?"

"Well, while you were up here, what were you supposed to do?"

Maud tilted her head. "I don't get what you're getting at."

"For example, were you supposed to give him information, you know, after the raid?"

"Information? What the blazes!"

"Isn't it possible? I have more reasons to think you're a spy than a hostage."

"I ain't a spy. You're looking to rile me."

"You speak greaser, don't you, some espanyol?"

"I can speak Spanish. I live in Mexico. What do you expect."

"America wasn't good enough for you? What are you, one of those Mormons?"

"I ain't a Mormon, and I ain't a spy."

"You live in one of those colonies down there. How many wives does your husband have?"

"You need to stop talking evil about my husband."

"You need to stop working for Villa."

"I'm talking to a post, ain't I. You can't hear a word."

Slocum straightened some papers on his desk, thoughtfully.

"You say you were taken from your ranch. Anybody else with you?"

"My husband and our hand, Frank."

"Where's Frank?"

"Dead, I reckon, with Ed."

"There's something funny about this. You say your husband and friend got killed, and you act like that's as normal as sunrise."

"By now, I suspect it is normal."

"Don't you have any reaction?"

Maud sat still, her hands folded in her lap.

"Well, you say you've been through all this. I got a whole town of women crying and pulling their hair out, but you're sitting here cool as a breeze, nothing but denials. I think inside your celebrating."

"I ain't a crying type."

"Aren't you human?"

"I'm my daddy's daughter. If it's any of your business."

Slocum became silent.

"If I was the crying kind of woman, I would've died of weeping. I learned not to."

Slocum nodded. "Anyone else out there with you?"

"You mean beside the Mexicans?"

"Beside the Mexicans. Other captives. As you say."

"There was a negro man. Mr. Spencer."

"First name?"

"Buck."

"He got taken captive?"

"Yes. Just like me."

Slocum narrowed his eyes.

"The same as you."

"I saw it happen to him. Except they didn't kill his family. Just left them in the house. Took the cattle, though. Like mine."

"I've talked to him."

"He's still alive? Well, that's some good news."

"What did he do during the raid? Was he a raider?"

"No, no, he was like me, taking care of the horses."

"Why'd you take care of their horses? You helped them with the raid. You assisted them."

"The horses didn't raid you. I'll take care of anybody's horse."

"How do you think he escaped?"

"I saw him roll away in the dust, playing possum."

"He escaped."

"Well, thank goodness."

"I wonder why he didn't ask permission to leave?"

"I can't explain that...doing that."

"Let's take a walk. You can walk, can't you?"

"Of course."

"Let's take a look at the town. Mary. Mary. We'll be back before lunch."

They walked together down the dirt street to the center of town, Slocum taking Maud's arm when she drifted away from him. On the main street, some buildings, the brick ones mainly, were untouched. Among them were heaps of blackened lumber, reducing to smoldering embers. The air was acrid with smoke and the stench of burning bodies. Slocum pointed to the remains, naming them.

"The bank."

"The Commercial Hotel."

"Dry goods."

Close to the camp, out in a field lay a dozen horses, dead. Maud looked at them. "Those aren't ours."

"Ours?"

"Villa's."

"No, they were ours. Your compañeros set fire to the stable."

"They're hard on horses. That's a fact. You think that was on purpose?"

"That's a hell of question, young lady."

"I don't think so. I don't think it was on purpose."

"What about the people they killed, every bit as defenseless."

"That was on purpose."

The stench of burning bodies was intolerable. At the end of the street was a large mound of debris smoking. They walked near it. "We killed about a hundred of the spics. And there they are." Slocum swept his arm toward the smoke.

Maud looked at the pile. Amid the smoldering lumber were smoking corpses, laid akimbo, arms, legs, strewn, heads hanging from slack, black necks. She squatted near the mound, peering into the confusion for tell-tale signs, a vest, a shirt, a hat, a shank of long, black hair. The fire had had destroyed any indicators. There were only blackened bits of textile, leathery, grimacing skulls, and limbs scorched to charcoal. Maud stood and walked away.

"Recognize anyone?"

Maud was quiet.

"Let's go back to the center of town."

They walked down the center of the dirt street. Maud's eyes ached and her throat was clenched tight.

"See that group of ladies over there?" Slocum pointed four women by the post office. "I want you to stand by them."

Maud furrowed her forehead. "Now what?"

"Just go over there. I'll be with you in a minute."

Maud walked toward them and stood nearby. They looked her over and turned away, absorbed in their conversation. One woman was weeping. Another stroked her temple, fiddling with her hair. She sobbed, holding her open hands out, her shoulders shaking. Maud watched her and began to tear up. She looked for Slocum. He had walked across the street to a small group of men. In their midst was a black man, talking to Slocum, nodding his head and pointing in her direction. Maud walked toward them.

"Say there, Buck."

"Hey, Maud. You made it through all right."

"Pretty much. You too."

"And take a look at you. You look like somebody's doll."

"Yes, the Colonel's wife has fixed me up. You could do with a bath, I'd say."

"Haven't gotten that far."

"The Colonel think you're a spy too?"

"Well, we haven't worked that out yet."

Slocum glowered. "This fellow has confirmed your story and you his. So that's enough of that."

"What are you going to do, Buck?"

"You mean where am I heading?"

"Yeah, you going back?"

"I don't know what else I can do? I can't leave my family down there. And the ranch. I couldn't manage that up here. How about you?"

"Leaving right now. I've got people over in Silver City. My folks are in Safford. I'll go to them, I guess. First, got to get my baby down in Pearson. If I have to walk there."

Slocum interrupted. "Maybe I can do something about that. Come on back to the house. I'm going to send a telegram."

"It's good to see you made it, Buck. Good luck to you."

"You, too, Maud. You too."

Maud spent the remainder of the morning waiting in Slocum's house, calmed by Mrs. Slocum's assurances. At lunch a young soldier came to the door. Slocum returned to the table.

"You're going to Arizona, correct?"

"Safford, in a bit. After I take care of my business."

"You have a horse and a couple of saddles."

"That's right. I want to keep them."

"We've got a freighter, a man named Peterson. He'll take your property to Safford. Free. He's volunteered to help you."

"That's very kind."

"There's something else. It takes a couple of hours to get to El Paso. You and Mary can take the afternoon train. Carranza is trying to be helpful. I think we can get Johnnie up there for you. But you'll need to leave now."

1960

ere, here. Stop here. This is the place. Coots Hill. This is where I watched the horses. Look, they've made a park out of it."

Johnnie braked the truck and pulled to the side of the road by the small rise.

Maud looked at the park sign. "Pancho Villa State Park, it says. Why would they name a park after him?"

"Let's get out."

Maud walked away from the pickup and looked around. Johnnie stood beside her.

"See, I was here, and this is where the horses were circled. I couldn't see much from here. Mainly, I just heard shots and screaming. I smelled gunpowder and fire."

"So this was a little safer."

"Sure, as long as I stayed here. My horse, my mule, caught a bullet, but only to its saddle, so it didn't get hurt. Scared me, though. So I stayed put."

Maud walked around the hill a way. Johnnie followed. "This is where the raiders rode into town and where they came back for fresh horses. They really got shot up bad. Some of them died right here. They were kids, you know, Indian boys, mainly. Especially now, I understand, they were more scared of Villa than they were of the army. He beat the blazes out of them sometimes."

She pointed toward town. "I saw a little boy, an American kid, running for his life away from town across there. It used to be a field. The boy, he was still in his long johns, running as hard as he could. In his underwear, and some of those raiders shooting after him. To me, that tells you a lot."

Maud dropped into silence, looking from the vantage at the town, now all concrete and asphalt, nothing as it had been. "The last time I was here, this place was an ash heap."

"It kind of surprises me, Ma, that you haven't been here since then."

Maud nodded. "Well, what would be the point? Anyway, Will doesn't much like to hear about this business."

"Why do you figure that is?"

"Don't know, really. Folks in Safford all knew about what happened to me, so when he met me, he must have already known. But if I talk "about it, he clams up. He told me once, 'That's enough about that.'"

"I wonder why it would bother him."

"Don't know, but when we moved to Mountainair, I don't think anybody knew about me being with Villa. Will likes it that way. I shut up about it tighter than a mason jar. By now, it's hard to twist it open and start talking."

They walked back to the truck. "Ma, let's get some lunch."

They drove to a little restaurant at the main intersection and sat across the table from each other.

"I'm sorry to say, I don't think the man cares for me much."

"What man?"

"Your husband, Will Medders."

"Is that so?"

"Yeah."

They sat silently for a bit, looking out the window at the traffic on the highway to Palomas, Mexico.

"He is a good man, Johnnie. I don't think he means harm."

Johnnie shrugged.

"Coming here is bringing back a lot of memories."

"I'll bet."

The waitress brought their enchiladas and coffee.

"They were good to me, you know."

"Who's that?"

"Villa's men."

"Good to you?"

"Yes, they really treated me well. They always took care that I had water and food. One or two in particular. I still think of them. They were very kind, most of them. Villa was good to me."

"I think my hearing's going bad. Say that again."

"Sounds strange to you."

"I think the years might have had a strange effect on your memory."

"I always felt that way." She bit into her food.

"Ma. Ma, they killed your husband, my father. That's right, isn't it?"

"Yes."

Johnnie laughed and shook his head.

"It's hard to explain. I'll tell you something I never told anybody."

"All right."

"About ten years ago, I was at Piñon Hardware."

"Don't know it, but go ahead."

"It's the hardware in Mountainair."

"Uh huh."

"And there was this old man outside, looked like a vagrant. A Mexican, I think. I didn't see his face."

Maud took another bite. Johnnie motioned with his hand for her to continue.

"The strange thing was, his boots. He was wearing Villa's boots, silver tips."

"How could that happen?"

"I think it was Villa. I mean, I thought maybe that Villa had come to check on me."

"In the fifties?"

"Does that sound silly?"

"Well, it sounds impossible. They shot Villa. You know that, don't you?

"Yes, I heard something about that."

"Back in the twenties."

"Are they sure it was him?"

"As sure as shooting."

"Because Villa was kind of tricky, you know."

"Ma, the man is dead."

Maud nodded.

"He wasn't checking on you. That wasn't him."

"Of course not. I was just imagining things."

"They shot him in his car. Many, many times. They took photographs to prove it."

"All right. Well, that's good to know, isn't it. And why would he be checking on me, anyway?" Maud laughed.

They ate in silence for a bit.

"You know who was good to me? The Slocums."

"The officer."

"Yes, but especially his wife. She cleaned me up like I was a baby. The man, he thought I was a spy, which I didn't appreciate. Not one bit. But afterwards they gave me clothes and some money. She came with me to El Paso, her and her maid. To get you."

"Where was I again?"

"The Morenos took care of you, but Maria took you to Pearson and told the authorities what had happened. You were a big shot."

"A big shot in Pearson?"

"Everywhere. You were in the newspaper. Carranza sent you up to me, the President of Mexico, himself."

"I remember that story. It's hard to believe now."

"They sent you up by a special train, this little boy. They said that Maria wouldn't give you up until she got official word from me. Because, you know, she promised me to take care of you. I had to send her a telegram telling her, OK, don't worry."

"I wish I could remember."

"You were two, younger. Anyway, I remember it very clearly. It was very official. They wouldn't let me take you without a photograph to document the event. It's a good picture. We were both smiling. You were so cute. Me, I looked as cooked as this hamburger. But it was so good to hold you again. I couldn't stop hugging you. I was so happy, I started crying. It was the first time in the whole time that I actually cried."

"You're a tough one, Ma."

"I suppose so. I was raised to be tough. It bothered people that I didn't cry. I think Villa wanted me to fuss and cry and cause a scene, to be weak. There was some very mean men always saying they were going to kill me. But I told them once, Go on, kill me if you got the nerve. Because, really, you know, I'd had enough. Slocum, too. He wanted me to cry to prove something."

"It is a wonder you're alive."

"Well, I made an impression on them. And on Villa, too. When he let me go he said, "Cursed is the man who is saddled with you.""

"That doesn't seem fair."

"It doesn't, does it? It's not my fault he kidnapped me. The main thing is, Villa was a man of his word. He let me go. I think he respected me because he couldn't break me."

"They should have known that the minute they saw you on a horse."

"Uh huh. Well, they gave me the right job, taking care of their herd. There were some days, I didn't think I would make it. We were so hungry and so exhausted. I thought I'd just drop dead. They had me riding a mule because they didn't trust me on a horse. You know but I like mules. After I realized I couldn't escape, realistically, I just did what a mule does."

"Kick people?"

"No, just put one hoof in front of the other. Sure footed, steady. No drama. Why would Villa call that cursed? I should have cursed him. That's what Buck wanted to do. Really, Villa, he was just a hooligan, him and his boys. Hooligans. They used a revolution as an excuse."

"I don't think you've made up your mind about that man. That's what I think."

They were driving back to Mountainair, the windows of the cab open, the wind whipping their faces. Across the northern horizon, grand cumulous clouds, monumental, nearly substantial, stacked one upon another, leaden and alabaster, framing the New Mexican sky. Rain fell in a grey shaft in the distance, evaporating before it reached the ground.

Maud rolled her window nearly all the way up again, a compromise between the heat and the wind. She slouched a little on the seat and rested her head against the back of the bench. Here eyes were closed. Johnnie looked over at her.

"Ma?"

"Yes, son?" She kept her eyes closed.

"It was terrible, what you went through, all you saw."

Maud smiled. "Uh huh."

"I just wonder, how did you get through it?"

"What do you think?"

"I don't know if I could have made it through that. I don't know? What gave you the strength?"

"You, sweetheart. You did."

Maud and her second husband Will Medders moved to Mountainair, New Mexico, shortly after they married in Arizona. They farmed pinto beans and then ranched cattle, raising seven children beside Johnnie. Maud continued to be an avid horsewoman until 1971. She was roping a steer calf when her horse reared, tossing her to the ground. She crawled to a nearby gate and pulled herself upright, resting against a post until help came. She complained that she did not want to go to the doctor, that it wasn't that bad an injury. But when she was taken to the hospital, the doctor said that her hip was broken, her ball joint shattered. He suggested she stop riding.

Maud wasn't much for airing grievances. She is reported to have said, "Complainin' don't make no pretty picture."

Will Medders died in 1965, survived by Maud until 1980, when she died December 25, aged 92.

READER'S GUIDE

January 10, 1916
1. Contrast the behavior of the rebels at the train hold-up when they are dealing with Mexicans and North Americans. What does that indicate about the purpose and intensity of their rebellion?

March 1
2. Why did the rebels gain by raiding the Wrights' ranch?

March 2
3. What attitudes do the characters evidence toward Villa and one another?
4. What does Villa's attitude toward the filmmaker indicate?

March 3
5. What plan is to be carried out during this journey? What are the several reasons for the plan?

March 4
6. What do Maud's reflections of her past conversations with Ed indicate about her upbringing and her current mood?

March 5

7. What does Maud's powerful reaction to the meat Palo offers her indicate about her state of mind?
8. What expectation does Villa have of Maud? What promise does he make to her?

March 6

9. What did Santa Teresita de Cobora offer the peasants of Mexico? Why would this bother the religious authorities? How might she have affected the early stages of the revolution?

March 7

10. How does Palo's extraordinary reaction to Teresita serve as a metaphor for the revolution that followed?
11. How do Buck's and Enriquita's sense of entitlement to the land differ?

March 8

12. What change in Villa's attitude is suggested by the American cowboy's familiarity and then death?
13. What emotions might Palo be experiencing when he makes himself available to Maud?

March 9

14. Why is Villa concerned about which direction Maud intends to go?
15. What is Maud's immediate inclination when confronted with the suffering of the Americans around her? What is the Americans' reaction to her?

March 10

16. Why does Colonel Slocum take Maud on a walk through Columbus, especially to have her stand near the grieving women?
17. What would motivate Carranza to act swiftly to return Johnnie to Maud?

1960

18. Of all Maud's recollections, the strangest is her imagining that Villa had come to Mountainair to check on her. What sense can the reader make of that?